CARNIVOROUS

by Rebecca Linquist

DORRANCE
PUBLISHING CO
EST. 1920
PITTSBURGH, PENNSYLVANIA 15238

Dorrance Publishing Co
585 Alpha Drive
Pittsburgh, PA 15238
Visit our website at *www.dorrancebookstore.com*

ISBN: 979-8-88925-091-3
eISBN: 979-8-88925-591-8

# ONE

People were milling around everywhere: some talking, some walking briskly, some looking at their smart phones. Just another normal day in a busy urban center, outdoors, surrounded by shops and restaurants, pigeons, occasional dogs and cats, and one woman activist.

Conspicuous by intention, Anna Hobart was standing in the middle of a busy plaza, with people passing all around her, carrying a sign that said: "Stop murdering animals." The sign itself was confrontational. It could have just as easily have had the words: "Be Vegan" on it, conveying the same sentiment, but it was no accident that Anna had chosen the words she had. If you asked her, she would tell you it wasn't to offend or annoy. She wanted change, and being passive and non-argumentative wouldn't yield the result she was after. Anna wanted people to react.

It didn't stop there. Anna wasn't your typical non-violent protester in any other way either. She was dressed in cougar-patterned lingerie: an underwire bra, a thong-style panty, complete with a garter, lace and high heels. Her hair was long, free, and fly-away, and she had carefully constructed her makeup to play up on her best features without being overdone; her hair highlights were violet in color and randomly placed as if an afterthought.

The disconnect with the masses was obvious, leaving anyone to wonder what the purpose was. If her true cause was to help defenseless animals, why was she clouding the issue with her own sexuality? Was she trying to attract men who wouldn't listen otherwise? Was it just about being provocative? Or did she simply miscalculate the effectiveness of her approach? One could only speculate.

The people milling around were a mix of college students, some teachers, and the general public: shoppers, tourists, some people in transit to work or home. To further get their attention, Anna had a recorder in her hand, and when people walked by, she would play an audio recording of animals making loud noises, presumably recorded in slaughterhouses or under crowded conditions in captivity where farm animals: pigs, cows, sheep or chickens were commonly confined in squalor to avoid any unnecessary expense when breeding them for human consumption.

The noises sounded like cows mooing loudly under distress, and Anna would play this and then shout, "If you're not vegan, you're killing animals needlessly. There is no reason for this. A plant-based diet can provide everything you need. You don't have to have blood on your hands. Have you seen the movie *Food, Inc.*? Have you been to dontwatch.org? Have you seen the film *Cowspiracy: The Sustainability Secret*? Inform yourself. You are killing innocent animals."

After doing this a few times, she'd typically catch the attention of a young man, generally in his twenties, and probably a college student. He'd just stare at her for a while, perhaps because of her provocative attire, and then he'd eventually work up the courage to engage with her.

He'd approach carefully, and say something like, "So, you don't think we should eat meat, but it's kind of hard to consistently find vegan food, and it's a little restrictive, don't you think?"

To which Anna would reply, "So you believe it's ok to eat animals because it's more convenient for you?" further provoking her target audience.

At this point, the guy, trying to disguise his leering at her body in her stripper-like costume would stumble around, look down and appear rattled, but he would always continue with something like, "It's just meat has a lot of protein, and everyone has been eating beef and chicken and milk forever, so giving all that up seems like a stretch."

It was always unclear to me what the guy was expecting. Did he just want to delay a little longer so he could keep checking her out for the free gawking? Or did he actually expect to develop some type of connection with her? Or maybe he was just so intrigued by the sheer audacity of someone being bold enough to stand around in public in her underwear that it kept him from moving on, but I suspected he was as intrigued by Anna as I was watching them.

I had discovered Anna when visiting San Francisco. Recently having graduated with my MBA, I was eager to take a break before settling down into a career that would force me to get serious for the rest of my life. I grew up back east and coming out to California to visit felt freeing. It was definitely one of the most liberal cities in the country, fondly or not-so-fondly referred to as a "sanctuary city", but despite the positive-sounding name, people calling it that usually weren't being complimentary. I had expected to see a lot of crazy things like open homosexuality at the Folsom Street Fair, famous for its kink, leather and public nudity, but this was something different all together. I got the feeling Anna wasn't from San Francisco at all.

Like me. We were both visiting. But unlike me, Anna was sure of herself. She had a mission.

At this point, Anna would say something to the guy who was still talking to her like, "Have you ever tried a whole foods, plant-based diet? We call it a WFPB diet, and it's got all the protein you need, and that way no animals would be sacrificed, brutally murdered, to put food on your plate. Don't you think that would be worth the change?"

I got the feeling that psychologically she was manipulating her target at this point. Let's face it, she had to know she was attractive, or she wouldn't be standing there in her underwear in front of everyone. She must have felt it gave her a leg up. It was almost like she was asking the guy out or angling for a dinner date with a dietary question that was so leading. I was surprised none of the guys I watched went in for the kill and asked her to accompany them somewhere to get to next base. Instead, most of them argued for some time, getting to a point where they disagreed with her, and then becoming more and more un-comfortable, the guy would take a walk. It was almost like she had re-jected him in some bizarre twist of events, and feeling rejected, he would excuse himself.

I expected to sit on that bench I found in the city for a short re-prieve and then hit some of the highlights of the city. I liked traveling by myself because I wasn't beholden to anyone, and after going straight through six years of college without a break, I felt I deserved some slack time.

Fortunately, affording it was no problem for me. My father was a wealthy businessman who owned real estate and capital all over the east coast, and the world. We spent time at our vacation home in the Hamptons, and we had an apartment in NYC, but we spent most of our time in Tampa, Florida, where Dad felt he was around his own kind: a large metropolitan area with professional sports teams (The Buccaneers, the Bandits, the Rowdies, and the Bay Rays, something for everyone, depending on what your favorite sport was), museums, dining and entertainment, but also quiet and safe. It was a laid-back beach community with a city life, but it didn't have near the panache and allure of San Francisco.

All the same, I hadn't expected to run into someone like Anna. I was drawn in emotionally as well as intellectually. I wasn't vegan, but I would consider it; more importantly, from a business perspective, there was something about the passion she put into her mission. I found my-self watching her interacting with a wide range of people, and each time she could out-argue them and out-reason them, and I wondered what made her tick. I was so enamored with the process of watching her that I let my plans to explore the city go for the time being so I could watch her work and get a sense of the dynamic.

At one point a woman in her forties walked up to her, and Anna started in as she always did, talking about the importance of animal rights, and the woman said to her, "You know animals die even when producing soybeans, like mice and moles and rabbits. They're just not as visible as cattle."

"I'm well aware of that," Anna defended her position, "but it's not the same as the continuous slaughter of cows, pigs, and chickens, and lots of other animals that are raped by artificial insemination, and their male babies are killed because they don't produce milk and more babies, and then the females are murdered after just a few years, not allowed to live out their natural life spans in peace."

At this point the woman looked at Anna's scantily-clad body, and she said, "You're worried about rape, and you're dressing like that?"

Anna became defensive, "What do you mean? Do you have a problem with how I dress?"

This was more amusing than a comedy to me, and it was free entertainment. I couldn't imagine what would come out of Anna's mouth next, but it wasn't wasted on me how her provocative nature was stirring up the crowd and bringing out their arguments, their contentious side, their fears, concerns, and knowledge gaps.

"I don't have a problem," the forty-something-year-old woman explained, "But don't you think it's a bit ironic that you're here preaching about abuse of animals and you're dressing in a sexual way? You seem to be suggesting women can't be taken seriously unless they demean themselves."

"What demeaning about this?" Anna seemed genuinely curious.

"Consider why you feel inclined to dress that way to make your point," the woman continued her argument, intent on exposing the idiosyncrasies of Anna's approach.

"I'm comfortable with my dress. I'm not sure how you can rationalize murdering innocent animals for your food," Anna insisted aggressively.

"Is there a question there?" the woman asked.

"The question is why not become vegan and save the animals? You can eat a plant-based diet and live without abusing animals! There's no reason to have blood on your hands!"

At this point, Anna hit the recorder play button in her hand, and the sounds of cows mooing raucously ensued. The forty-something-year-old woman walked away with a downward wave of her hand, unconvinced.

I was feeling playful at this point, and I started to wonder what would happen if I approached Anna. What tack should I take, and how would she respond? I decided that being too eager to accept her theories on veganism wouldn't give her enough of a challenge, and being too confrontational wouldn't distinguish me from the others, so I meandered over to her and waited until she turned towards me with her sign.

"You're a friend to animals," I stated as I approached.

"I am," she said, nothing to argue about.

"What do you think it's going to take to change people's minds?" I thought it was a legitimate question.

"Awareness," she answered matter-of-factly, "People need to understand they have the blood of animals on their hands."

Now it was time to introduce some lack of total agreement.

"You don't think people know that?" I asked, as genuinely as I could possibly be.

"I think they do, but people are hypocrites. Are you a hypocrite?"

I should have known she'd go direct and come after me. She was on to my tack.

"Most of us are in some ways. I understand. You're saying people know it's wrong, but they just go on doing it anyway, and you want to bring so much attention to the issue that people can't continue doing it without experiencing a moral conflict within themselves," I summarized what I believed her philosophy to be. That was deep, even for me.

"That's right. If you bring enough attention to something, people have got to come to terms with their own reality to make sense of it. That's where we need to go to create change. Have you seen *Foods, Inc.?* or *Dominion* on You Tube? Or *dontwatch.org?* or *Cowspiracy: The Sustainability Secret*, the movie? Film and videos show you the real story."

"And I'm sure it's ugly. I wonder who really wants to watch that."

"No one wants to, but if you go there, you'll understand that veganism is the only choice."

I admired her tenacity, her strength, her passion. I wanted to ask her out for a veggie burger, but instead, I just said, "So how can I learn more about this? The activism part, not just the videos on abuse."

"You could come tonight and see the response I get."

"The response? What's tonight?"

"I'm making an appearance at a steakhouse."

That was an offer I couldn't refuse.

# TWO

I showed up early, and I can't really say why. I don't know if I intended to order a steak dinner and try to finish it before Anna arrived, or what my initial thought was, but when I got there, I purely took notice of how jovial and upscale the environment was. It actually wasn't just a steakhouse, but beef was definitely on the menu. Anna had chosen a fine dining venue where most tables were occupied by a couple, possibly on a date or celebrating a special event like a birthday or anniversary, and there were candles to make it light enough to see the menu because the restaurant was quite dark.

I got a table for one, and being somewhat ahead of the most popular dining hour scored myself a table without a reservation. I was drinking in the environment, relishing in those moments of calm before the storm, noticing what people were wearing, how they were behaving, and what food was being served before it would all be disrupted.

I scanned the menu looking for something enticing, finding that meat just didn't seem appealing given the circumstances, but it was hard to find something that didn't have chicken, seafood or beef on the menu. I settled for a salad and butternut squash ravioli entrée, which was never a go-to choice for me, but somehow seemed like the obvious one given the anticipated upcoming event.

I found myself feeling nervous and anxious near the "witching hour" when Anna had told me she planned to make her entrance. I hadn't ever seen an activist barge into a dining establishment, and I was somehow excited and intrigued at a deep level. Her presence and people's reactions had already become addictive.

At one point during my solo dinner, I was so distracted by the ambience, the edgy jazz, the dressed-to-impress clientele, the bartender's exquisite mixed drinks passing by my table raised high on cocktail trays by waiters eager to present them at their customers' tables, the whispers of overheard conversations with bits of laughter, bursts of coughing, and sounds that carried with shifts in volume, overlapping other conversations at the pause points.

The waitress was a middle-aged woman with prominent, stylized glamour eye glasses in an animal pattern, reminding me that Anna's visit was imminent, and I began to anticipate it once again. She inquired how my meal was tasting, and I responded that I'd like a glass of wine, mostly to delay the check arriving, although she didn't pressure me to give up my table, surprisingly, given the fact that the restaurant was filling with diners by the minute. I noticed there wasn't a free table, and there appeared to be a number of guests filling the bar area and the waiting area, the noise level increasing, as they waited patiently for a table.

Several minutes later, I heard an uproar. There was a scuffling of chairs and indescribable furniture and wall noises, as though people were scrambling to move away quickly from something, brushing their backs and bodies against the walls and shoving the tables and chairs in the bar area to the side; and then she emerged, dressed only in a skin-colored G-string, apparent from the line of the material connecting in the back as she turned, and drenched in blood on her entire upper body. Her hair hung freely and haphazardly, draped over her shoulders and down her back, and her eyes were livid, raging, intense. She had on a garter belt and a lacy garter on her right leg, stained with blood.

Anna made her way through the restaurant, pacing at an even gait, as she spoke loudly and clearly without a microphone, "If you are eating meat, you are contributing to the murder and abuse of animals," she said matter-of-factly as she continued to walk through the restaurant, taking one aisle at a time, passing the patrons and scanning the room, without making concentrated eye contact with any one individual for too long, "Could you do it yourself?" she asked, provocatively, "Could you take the blade to their throats, ending their lives? Could you cut them open, gut them, and let them bleed out? Or do you just let someone else do it for you while you eat in gourmet restaurants where you feel safe and protected?"

By this point, some of the restaurant employees were getting visibly shaken. The waiters were moving away from her to the sidelines. One man, who appeared to be in a management role, started walking up to her, brushing against her arm when he got close, as if to restrain her, but perhaps realizing that since she was virtually naked, he would have to touch her with more intimacy than he was comfortable with to prevent her from continuing. He kept his distance.

All the while, Anna appeared unaffected by the audience's reactions. She maintained the same stable voice quality, as she maneuvered through the tables, launching the same accusations with the same, unwavering candor, and I would have expected nothing less.

The manager, still the only one attempting to stop her, decided to become more forceful. He yelled out, "It's time for you to leave, ma'am," which seemed unnecessarily polite, given the circumstances, perhaps as a way of showing that he was being respectful while she was not.

Perhaps he was concerned with what people would think if he manhandled her in an effort to get her to leave.

"You have to get out!" he continued to shout, but by this time, Anna was playing the recorded animal noises again, the "MOOOOO" sound emerged in a raging, deep guttural sound, clearly from a slaughter house, and some of the other tortured animal noises were no less troubling, disturbing, and annoying.

"Shut that damn thing off!" the manager shouted, his rage getting the best of him.

Anna continued to stride fluidly and effortlessly through the restaurant, carefully turning so everyone could see the blood on her chest, something like a pastie affixed to each of her nipples, with the rest of her breast covered in the bloody substance, which most people assumed was blood, although I had my doubts. Was it ketchup? Was it food coloring? Was it paint?

Her rhetoric continued as well, "Non-human animals deserve to live. Instead, they are being abused and you are eating them, contributing to their abuse. If you are not eating vegan, you are funding their rape, mutilation, and abuse. Did you know their babies are killed? Did you know they live in despicable environments where they are overfed and filled with antibiotics so they can provide more meat for you to eat? How does that make you feel?"

She made her way through the aisles a second time, sometimes facing the bar, so all the restaurant employees taking cover would see her as well, "You who work in this establishment, how do you live with yourselves? Most people love animals. Most of us have cats and dogs as pets at home. How do you rationalize the difference? Would you kill your pet for something to eat? Would you take your cat or dog to be sliced up and sold at a restaurant? If not, you are a hypocrite to let innocent cows be brutally murdered to furnish you with a bloody steak!"

Anna's rage was apparent, but her pacing perpetuated in its methodical execution: one step after another, the blood stains on her feet visible inside of the stilettos she pranced around in, her glute muscles flexing as she walked, her hair waving in the breeze; there was a freedom to her actions. As offensive, off-putting, annoying, and inappropriate as many in the audience of restaurant employees and customers were, her actions imparted a sense of truth, conviction, righteousness that was impossible to ignore. The effect was bone chilling, and I was mesmerized.

At one point, I felt she might have seen me, recognized me from earlier when we had first met at the outdoor venue where she was arguing with passersby at will, equally naked, similarly engaging, completely uninhibited and unrestricted, hell bent on her messaging. Be vegan or be held accountable. It was as simple as that.

I wanted her to see me, recognize me, have some connection with me. I wanted to be part of her confident march on injustice without having to risk anything, but it didn't work that way. She never made direct eye contact with me. Was that intentional?

The majority of onlookers were frozen with terror, and I was captivated by their immediate reactions. Many looked away and fell silent, waiting for "someone to do something", not wanting to provoke her further or involve themselves in the act. Yet they were a captive audience, and there was nothing they could do about it other than leave the restaurant, which was not a move I noticed anyone making. In some sense, I wondered if people were merely waiting to see what she would do next.

"There is blood on your hands, and in your stomachs, and yet you have a choice!" At this point, she threw blood onto the floor, or what appeared to be blood, and all eyes followed the spilling, as she dribbled it down the corridor so that all tables had eyes on her and then looked away in disgust.

The police arrived shortly afterwards, and she was arrested. Anna didn't resist arrest. She had this fixed expression on her face, and her body went limp, and one of the officers threw what looked like a large coat around her shoulders as they escorted her out. I was left to wonder: what would be her next performance? I knew I had to be there.

Three

I didn't see Anna for a while, and I missed her. I walked through the streets of San Francisco, the same locations as before, but I didn't see any protesters of any kind. There were tourists, shoppers, visitors galore, but no one for animal rights or any other controversial topic trying to make a difference. The effect she had had on me became profound.

I decided to go about my business, visiting the Ansel Adams exhibit at SFMOMA, the Museum of Modern Art, and I spent the morning there, enjoying my café latte and croissant and playing tourist, but try as I might to engage myself with other topics, my mind kept drifting back to Anna. Not just her body, covered in blood, but also her dedication to animals, her resolve to do whatever it took to make a difference, and her ability to conquer fear and do something that had probably landed her in jail.

I realized I would be distracted permanently until I found out what happened to her. I took out my smart phone and ran some searches, but knowing no more than her name didn't bring anything up. Then I searched on arrests and incidents and even the name of the restaurant where I saw the cops arrest her, but I couldn't find anything. I thought of trying to figure out where people were taken when there were arrests in San Francisco, but it was a big city, and I figured no one was going to tell me anything. Ultimately, I let it go. I had my own life to get back to, and I couldn't waste more time on a clueless, albeit determined and resourceful, young woman who intentionally put herself in harm's way and suffered the consequences.

I got on the plane and went home to Tampa with a plan to start applying for jobs in NYC and exploring opportunities now that I had my MBA. I reached out to my friend and confidante, Carl Olsen, and we met up for booze, comfort food, and catching each other up on the latest in our lives.

"Hey," Carl said, grabbing a stool and pulling up next to me at the sports bar.

"Hey, yourself," I responded, combing the menu for my choice in beer and settling on a Stella Artois.

"Should we get some appetizers? Buffalo wings?" Carl prompted.

I found myself cringing at the thought of eating abused chicken.

"I was thinking ..."

"Rocky Mountain oysters?" Carl prompted.

"No, no," I was getting ugly visuals of fried bull testicles, and imagining Anna's reaction, covered in blood; what disgusting things would she say or do about that?

"I was thinking nachos," I said emphatically.

"Works for me," Carl agreed, "The works?"

I knew he meant with ground beef on top.

"Just cheese and hot sauce."

"Ok, dude, but you seem a little uptight," he remarked.

I decided to take the conversation in a different direction, "Yeah, I am. I need to find the right job opportunity now, and I guess I've been so buried in study, I didn't line something up."

"You'll have no problem with your connections," he pointed out.

By that, Carl meant my dad. Dad knew everyone.

"You're probably right about that," I relented, thinking I'd rather find something on my own. I didn't want to think about the ramifications of letting Dad control my destiny. We had a strong father-son bond, but he was a self-made man, and I wanted to be one, too.

"Anyhow, do you have any interest in venturing up to the city with me?"

By this, Carl was understood to mean NYC. We often went there for the excitement that living in Florida could never provide.

"What are you thinking?" I wanted to know if he meant the fooling around, we used to when we were younger or something more related to my job search.

"I'm up for anything, bro," he said speculatively, "strip clubs, fine dining, networking with some of the big guys – you name it."

I knew Dad could turn me on to some of his buddies who might be recruiting new MBAs, and it was a good excuse to get out of my head. I kept thinking about Anna and SF, and I wanted to get refocused, which had been the whole intention behind going out of town in the first place.

"Let's do it," I committed, "It'll be good for both of us to lighten up a bit."

Carl knew I meant myself, but he didn't say anything. Carl was nothing if not laid back and accommodating.

We settled in to watch the Buccaneers play the Panthers and down a few brewskis with our nachos.

Before I left for NYC, I sat down with Dad in his office. He was jostling some papers around on his desk and seemed distracted.

"Dad, you need to get automated. No need for all that paper any-more," I prompted. Dad

always had a multitude of projects going on at the same time, and his idea of using computer technology didn't extend beyond using the calendar on his iPhone.

"Old dog ... no new tricks," he commented offhandedly, "What do you need, son?"

"Getting ready to hit NYC next week. Just thought you might have some ideas for my job search."

"Great place to start, glad you asked, Daniel. One of my contacts deals in prime meats there. You should hook up with him when you're in the city. His name is Don Price. I'll email you his contact info," Dad gave me the full download as if he was ready to move onto his next "think piece."

Prime Meats? I didn't know Don, and normally I would just take Dad's advice, but ever since Anna, I was thinking about things in a different way. I knew better than to ask Dad about it. He hated being questioned when he made a recommendation.

He used to say, "You do *everything* for them, and they never appreciate it," when referring to his protégés, so I didn't dare ask him to clarify. I'd need to source this out on my own.

"Thanks, Dad," I replied instead.

"Sure," he had already moved onto something else, trying to reconcile a note on a piece of paper with something in his email, "I'll send you a message with other recommendations," he continued.

Recommendations. That was good. I didn't have to take him up on everything; they were just recommendations.

I did some digging on interviewing and job leads, and sure enough, there were several opportunities: one with a bank, but I wasn't sure I wanted to work for a bank, and I had a lead on a management job and a financial analyst job. I shot them all emails, mentioning I would be in the city and would like to have a discovery interview if that was an option, and then I scheduled the flight. Carl and I liked to stay at the Waldorf Astoria whenever we were in the city, so I made a reservation and shot Carl an email to make his. All set!

But my mind kept floating back to San Francisco and Anna. I pondered why this woman had had such a profound impact on me. I had always felt like I "went along to get along", but Anna had strong convictions. She fought for what she believed in. She inspired me, intrigued me, and mesmerized me. I was becoming addicted to her activism, and I realize now that this is when my obsession first began. I couldn't put her out of my mind.

Once in the city, Carl and I breathed a sigh of relief. We loved the energy, the electricity, the complexity. We'd been coming to New York since we were kids, and although our tastes in venue had changed, the city never disappoints. We took a cab to the Waldorf in midtown Manhattan and left our luggage with the bellman, and then we took a cab to my first appointment with Don Price, dad's friend, in lower Manhattan in the Financial District. He had invited the two of us for drinks near his office.

Carl and I both took in the city: the sky scrapers, the ambience, the hustling pace. It was more energetic and alive than low-key Tampa. Carl was an accountant, and he worked for himself. He had several companies who hired him to do their books. He hadn't gotten an MBA. He was too laid back and practical for continued education, but we'd known each other since grade school and bringing him along to meet Don just made good sense.

We got to the bustling cocktail lounge just down the street from Don's office where he wanted to meet us. Carl and I got a table and ordered beers and hung out. Don arrived a few minutes later, carrying his jacket over his arm, a newspaper splayed out on the same arm, which looked like the Wall Street Journal, and his smart phone in the other, juggling all the moving parts.

"Hey," he said, positioning himself at our table, "You look just like your dad," he said to me, presumably to explain how he found us so quickly without asking the hostess.

"That's what everyone tells me," I confided, and it was true. I had a softer look, but my dad's features, dark green eyes, fine dark hair and medium height with a certain steadfastness made it so everyone saw the resemblance at first glance.

He turned to Carl, "And you're the accountant?" he asked, shaking Carl's hand.

"I am; been friends with Dan and his dad for the last twenty years."

"Good," Don declared, setting up his portion of the table like his office, situating his phone to the right and his paper to the left, his jacket on the back of his chair in a take-charge manner.

"Glad you guys could make it. Kind of an informal interview, but honestly, Daniel, your dad has told me a lot about you, and I think you're the right fit for what I need."

That was the double-pronged skewer of having a powerful dad. It opened a lot of doors, but I also wanted to open my own doors.

Don motioned to the waitress and ordered himself an extra dry martini and then turned towards the two of us, making the small round cocktail table into his executive launch pad, "I'll cut to the chase, and then you two can ask me any questions you have," he began, "I'm running a private equity firm. I know you're both intimately familiar with what that is, but I wanted to clarify things a bit so you can understand the pain points."

My dad did the same thing: private equity firm basically meant you invest in other companies, and by doing so, you get some say in how things are run, but there's a fine balancing act between getting involved without getting overly entrenched in the details and staying so distant and uninvolved that you lose touch. Navigating that balancing act along with choosing wisely the timing of when to buy, when to sell and what businesses to buy was a science but more of an art. At least, that was what my dad had taught me over the years.

"Your dad," Don was clarifying, "is more of a holding company. He's been in the game so long he doesn't really focus on that three to six year turnaround time to get profit up and sell off a business that you buy into. He's more of a slow burn, and I'm more of a quick turn. Does that make sense?"

"Sure," I responded for both Carl and me; it was more of a rhetorical question.

"Let's get down to the meat and potatoes," Don cut to the chase, "I've got a number of organizations to track, and I'm spread too thin. I'm planning to stick to the big picture stuff," he did a curt side nod towards the WSJ copy to his left, "and focus on selecting companies and timing the buys and sells, but I need you boys to run the private equity business, checking in with the companies, looking at the books, giving them guidance and directions and just overseeing the mechanics of it and reporting back to me."

He paused and looked at us for engagement. Both Carl and I were attentive and interested.

"Go on," I probed, leaning forward, "I'd like to know more about what companies you manage, what stages they are at, and what you need."

"Of course," he handed Carl and I some printed reports, reminding me of Dad's generation, not going paperless any time soon, but using technology to some extent.

"You'll get an idea from these: P&L statements, projections, business plans. I've detailed net profit, sales and revenue growth, debt level in some cases, profit margin and free cash flow. In the beginning, there will be a little preparation work, but I think once the two of you set up a system, you'll be able to do a lot of this from Florida and just come up to NYC a few times a year to be in person, except ..."

He hesitated a bit, which piqued both of our interests.

"Yes ..." Carl encouraged further exploration.

"It's the prime meats thing that concerns me the most right now," he stated. This gave me a flashback to my dad's comment when he first suggested I contact Don.

"What's that about?" I asked curiously.

"Well, consumers are getting pickier about their meat, you know, the cuts, the quality, grass-fed, free range, all that stuff, and there's a big market for high end meat, the prime cuts, so I'm involved in that sector: the specialty meat market from slaughter to delivery to restaurant and

deli. Here in NYC, we have some fantastic signature bistros, and I've bought into several organizations that work together to deliver quality and perfection, at a price," he finished.

"Of course," Carl commented, more engaged than I was. I was thinking of Anna and how disparate Don's goals were from hers.

"So, you want us to get involved and see if we can get these prime meat organizations working seamlessly together?" Carl paraphrased and confirmed.

"That's it; I knew you boys would get this. We need to work on streamlining, and I'd like the two of you to stop by one of these signature bistros while you're in town, have dinner there, talk to the management and get the feel for the place."

We both smiled, Carl more vigorously than I, but we were both intrigued.

"You see, there's a lot going on in the prime meats arena, but there is diversity in my portfolio, so you can look at the facts and figures there, and I'll also email you what you need to look at, but I wanted to get a sense of whether this is the right fit for you both. Dan, I'd like you to head this up and be my right hand man to run the business in my absence as my key liaison, and Carl, I'd you to run with the accounting function for all the companies. Does that sound like what the two of you are interested in?"

I knew Carl would deflect to me, and honestly, I had no qualms about working with Don, especially since Dad made the referral, and I really didn't relish having to dig deep, spending hours sourcing companies and interviewing. Why not take a bird in the hand?

"It sounds like a great opportunity, Don. We haven't talked about compensation," I commented, knowing we needed to get our chips on the table.

"Glad you asked," Don replied, taking another couple of sheets of paper out of a satchel he had managed to carry along with all the other moving parts, "These are agreements for you and Carl to look over. I think you'll find the terms and conditions favorable."

I was surprised because there had been no previous mention of salary. I handed the accountant one to Carl and took a look at mine. Not only was the salary more than generous, there were provisions for bonuses and profit sharing, full health insurance coverage, and the hours were flexible. It was definitely a good fit for me.

"When do you want us to start?" I asked.

"ASAP, boys. Take a day or so to look it over, and if it works for you, just sign and text the agreements back to me."

Carl was looking at his document as we were finishing our beers when I spotted her. The bar had a second floor with a winding staircase, and a pair of black stiletto heels was heading down to the main floor where Don, Carl and I were seated. There was something about those heels and the stride of the woman walking in them that drew my attention. They were familiar, and as more and more of her materialized, her long athletic legs, her form fitting professional black sheath dress as she slowly came around the corner of the winding staircase. Her bright red silk blazer caught my eye, and her shoulder length black hair, cascading and flowing along with her gait transfixed me, but once I saw her bright blue eyes as she rounded the corner and inescapably looked right at me, there was no mistaking her. It was Anna.

I felt a sense of awe and deep comfort. I had been thinking about her, obsessing about her so much that it almost felt surreal to see her now. As odd and serendipitous as it was, it felt natural. I had felt like I'd never see her again after leaving San Francisco, although it made no sense that there should be any expectation I would. I could only question whether she would recognize me. After all, we'd had no real conversation or engagement, not at the outdoor protesting event or the restaurant where she was arrested. We'd had a few lines of conversation at the protest, but she had talked to hundreds of people; was I all that memorable? I couldn't be sure.

As she walked towards us, I began to realize that if I didn't say something she might walk right on by, and it might be our only chance to connect with each other. I didn't want to blow destiny, and I was working up the courage to say or do something; I just wasn't sure what. Then the unexpected happened.

"Anna!" Don said, "There's someone I'd like you to meet."

Astonished that Don knew her, my eyebrows raised up dramatically, but I said nothing and let things unfold.

Anna stopped at our table, and Don said, "These two men are your new conduits to me. This is Dan, he's the primary one, and he'll be running the operation."

Don paused, and Anna's eyes settled on me. Did she recognize me? Did Don know she was an animal rights activist? Did it matter?

I thought I caught a glance of indignation; not fear, not outright anger, just perhaps a lack of trust and a reason for concern, and then she recovered in a split second. A smile crossed her face from ear to ear, and she said, "Charmed!" extending her arm, and her beautiful well-manicured nails extended out for me to shake her hand.

"And this is Carl," Don continued, as she locked eyes with me and held my gaze. I didn't want to let go, but Carl stood up and waited patiently for what must have felt like an eternity. She didn't break contact; I did, but it was only because it felt awkward to keep holding her hand so long.

"Good to meet you, Anna," Carl said decisively, and then shook hands, short and fast, up and down, nothing like the connection I had made with her: long, lingering, profound.

"These two are going to work directly with you to make sure the prime meat selection at the restaurant goes well; that things improve, expand, and revenue increases, of course, along with customer satisfaction," Don explained.

This led to further confusion for me. Who was Anna? An animal rights activist involved in growing the prime meat business in NYC? The contradiction defied logic.

Don stood to leave and clarified the confusion, at least from his perspective, "Anna is the manager of the restaurant. She'll make sure the two of you get all the information and cooperation you need. I suggest you have dinner there tonight, men, and I look forward to our continued relationship," he shook our hands; we muttered words of agreement, acceptance, and understanding, and Don walked out, leaving the three of us at a stand-off.

Carl filled in the gap for my silence and asked Anna, "What time do you suggest for dinner?"

"7 pm would be perfect," she said, smiled, shook both of our hands again, and exited.

I was at a loss for words.

27

I was at a loss for words.

❧Four

Dinner at the NYC Steakhouse was an interesting experience. We arrived at 7 pm, and due to the awkwardness and ambiguity of the situation, I elected to keep Carl in the dark. I didn't necessarily have to tell him about the animal rights demonstration and the arrest experience. I could keep it to myself for now and see how things progressed, buying myself some time to make sense of things.

The décor was exceptional: sparkling clean, bright, well decorated and understated. The tablecloths were black and simple with small electronic candles on all the tables. The menu had a vast array of prime meat beef choices: rib-eyes in two sizes (ten or twelve ounces), prime rib, filet mignon, porterhouse, and, of course, the infamous New York strip, top sirloin, and smash burgers on brioche buns, even gourmet beef sliders as appetizers.

I was considering what to order when I realized I didn't want meat. I began to wonder if it was possible to order anything vegan there and what our waiter would say if we asked. I had hoped Anna would wait on us personally, but she wasn't anywhere within line of sight when we entered, and we had been seated in a blond waitress' section who suggested we peruse the menu with the promise of a swift return.

Carl spoke to me first, "You doing all right, bro? Thought you'd be more stoked about this," he remarked, obviously genuinely surprised.

"I'm all good, just taking it easy, treading lightly. We'll see how it goes."

Actually, I was scouring the menu for a vegetarian entrée. I would eat meat, but somehow after my experiences over the last couple of weeks, it just wasn't where my mind or stomach was at.

The waitress returned and said, "I'm Geneviève, and I'll be serving you tonight. I'm told you are very special guests. You'll be overseeing the place soon?" she inquired.

"In a sense," Carl responded, "Our boss wants us to check out the cuisine."

"You've come to the right place for that!" she exclaimed with a large, fake smile on her face. I wondered how waitresses stay motivated to ask the same questions over and over again, but then the restaurant business was new to me.

"We have all kinds of steaks," Geneviève informed us. She even brought a large laminated card with her that pictured the outline of a cow, and all the cuts of meat were delineated on it. As she was taking us through it, she explained what the options were on the menu.

I decided to be bold and asked, "What do you have besides meat?"

Carl shot me a perplexed look. I figured I could explain to him later that it was a good idea to get the lay of the land by asking questions that weren't obvious to see how they responded. Of course, my motive wasn't that, but he would likely let it go with my excuse as a plausible explanation.

Geneviève took a moment to think through the most politically correct answer, and then she hedgingly began, "You could start with a French onion soup, and a salad, and we could do some vegetable side dishes." She was struggling and attempting to come up with an acceptable answer.

Anna came up behind her with a wide smile, and while I hadn't seen her coming, her entrance was not discreet. Her hair was more stylized than usual, pulled back in a tasteful bob, and she was wearing the same black sheath of earlier with the same red silk blazer, but she captivated me all the same.

"Are you boys looking for something vegetarian?" she paused and seemed genuinely interested in our response.

Carl got a little defensive. "I want to try your steaks; I mean, that's what you're known for, right?" he asked.

Anna smiled, paused, looked at me and said, "It's not what I'm known for."

There was a large lump in the back of my throat. I wasn't sure how to respond, and I couldn't believe she'd say that in her situation, risking blowing her cover as an animal rights advocate, but what did I know?

"This isn't a steakhouse known for its steak?" Carl was getting more belligerent than I had ever experienced him to be. It made me chuckle. Anyone who could get a rise out of Carl deserved some notice.

"It most certainly is," Anna quipped, "And steak you shall have. I'll let Geneviève tell you all about it, but before I go," she hesitated flirtatiously, and I thought I saw her lick her lips, "I wonder if your partner, here, Dan, is it? Wouldn't prefer an alternative to meat?"

"I would," I answered without hesitation, "What are the options?"

"Sadly, not a whole hell of a lot," Anna said, lingering her pause even longer for effect, "But maybe you boys can do something about that since you're going to be reporting directly to the big guy and all that."

Carl looked utterly confused, and I felt compelled to bring him in on our shared secret, but something kept me from disclosing the whole story, especially in public forum.

"We should talk about it," I said to salvage the moment, "I hear they make cauliflower steaks now."

Anna smiled with her expected long, wide, extended lip reach, and boldly announced, "Oh, you don't know the half of it."

The inside joke had gone far enough. Carl was starting to feel excluded, confused, even possibly angry with me, but I knew I could still turn it around. I wanted to stay in it a little longer, just to see where it might go.

"What's your favorite item on the menu, Anna?" I asked, feigning naiveté.

"Blood rare prime rib," she said, "Dripping in blood."

Carl fidgeted in his seat, and he seemed uncomfortable.

"Do you say that to customers?" he asked Anna.

"Dan's no customer," she explained, "He's the boss, right?"

I smiled at her, "I think I like being your boss. Why don't you just bring me something you know I'll love to eat?"

She met my gaze and held it, "They won't allow that in this restaurant," she said, and she walked away.

Carl shot me a contemptuous look.

Geneviève took our order. I did order the French onion soup, salad, and a pasta side dish. Carl ordered a NY strip, but he seemed irritated, and under his breath he said, "Jesus."

"Carl? Does this bother you?" I asked.

"We'll talk later," he said, and I knew for a fact he'd let me have it before we reached the curb.

The rest of the dinner was uneventful. We ate; we talked; we went back to the kitchen and met some of the staff: the chef, the sous-chef, a few other employees and did the due diligence of scrutinizing the place so we could give a full report to Don.

As soon as we hit the door, Carl lit into me, "What the HELL was that all about? You and that Anna chick?"

I knew better than to cover it up entirely and play innocent, so I settled for second best.

"I guess I'm just lonely since things didn't work out with Carol," I said calmly.

I knew the world's smallest violin wouldn't play for me forever, but Carl did have some compassion left in him around the long-term relationship I had that had fizzled out last year and that I obviously hadn't recovered from yet.

"I get that," Carl replied as we walked back to the Waldorf. We both needed the exercise, and it wasn't a long walk, "But do you have to mix your sex life with business?"

"Are you trying to tell me I shouldn't shit where I eat?" I poked the bear.

Carl guffawed, "Oh, yeah, the old Dan is back."

I joined in the revelry, and the two of us went back to the hotel to sync up on the documents Don had given us and to talk about how we wanted to proceed. We spent hours poring over the numbers and the data in the reports, Carl pointing out that from an accounting perspective, the prime meats gig looked lucrative with potential for future growth.

"The only thing is," Carl said, "I'm not sure your heart is in this."

"My heart?" I asked, thinking about how much I was obsessing over Anna and wondering what Carl would think if he only knew the whole story.

"I mean you didn't have a steak tonight," he challenged.

"Ah, that's what's bothering you. Well, I might as well let you know; I'm trying to lose weight. I'm getting a little chunky, and maybe the ladies are noticing, and that's why I haven't had a date lately. It's putting me off my game."

"Dude!" Carl countered, "Eating French onion soup and all that pasta crap you had tonight; that's not gonna help you lose weight."

"You're probably right," I acquiesced too easily and too soon, "We're in this together. We'll figure it out."

Carl always went for the arguments where I suggested our friendship could overcome anything. Mostly because it could.

I lay awake in my luxury studio listening to soft relaxation music piped through the high-end speakers at the Waldorf, drinking a glass of Macallan premium single malt whiskey from the private collection my room had to offer, wondering who Anna really was. What was her game? I had thought she was just an animal rights activist with a strong head on her shoulders, but now to discover that she was a savvy business woman, outspoken as all get out, and elegant too? It was mind boggling.

And what about Carl? I was going to take a new job with Carl as my partner, and I didn't want things to go sideways. Carl and I had been through crazy times together: Everything from getting bullied and standing up for each other to doing each other's homework to avoid failing grades. I didn't want to risk our relationship for a woman I didn't even know.

And that was another thing – the job. Don Price was Dad's friend, and Dad had gotten me this job. A lot was riding on this. I didn't want to do anything stupid and blow it. This was my first job since getting my MBA, and I'd spent a lot of time in school and in internships, but I hadn't held a job for years, and I didn't want to get this wrong and have to start over in some entry level position that wouldn't lead anywhere for years. This job paid well and had a lot of potential. It wasn't just prime meat. Don owned several companies in different fields, and I could explore all of that, and if I impressed him with my business acumen, he'd probably let me choose what company he bought next. This could be a great career for me if I didn't blow it.

I fell asleep realizing that although all these concerns were real, I just wanted to get to know more about Anna, regardless of the risk.

FIVE

Back in Florida, Dad was pleased that Don had called him and let him
know we were working together. I got home late the night before, and
I hadn't gotten a chance to touch base with Dad. We lived together in
Tampa in one of Dad's properties. Mom and Dad weren't divorced, but
Mom preferred to live in upstate New York and to visit her relatives in
Maine, so she stayed in another one of Dad's properties. That suited
him fine because Dad was basically a loner. He missed her incredible
cooking, but he was satisfied with takeout to protect his freedom. That's
probably where I got my personality of being aloof, disconnected and
easy going, but it wasn't necessarily serving me well. I lacked the conviction I saw in Anna. I wanted to be more like her, and I was drawn to
her like a magnet.

Dad came up behind me at the coffee maker on the counter in
our kitchen.

"So ... tell me about the job," he prompted.

I jumped. "Sneaking up on me?" I asked, taking my time to recover,
and then I replied, "It's a great opportunity, and Carl and I are going
for it."

"That's great to hear," Dad said, looking proud and supportive, as
he leaned on the counter and munched on a bagel.

"I hear from Carl that there's a hot one up there for you," Dad continued to taunt me.

"Oh, so you're talking to Carl first now, huh? Before you ask me
about the job?" I acted more upset than I was.

"Carl called me about an accounting gig he's doing for me, and I just asked him in passing about your trip to NYC. He said there was a hot gal managing that steakhouse up there that you have a thing for, that's all."

"I don't have a 'thing' for her, Dad, but yes," I acknowledged, "She's attractive."

"Don't wait too long," Dad said, heading back to his office, "Your young rugged good looks won't last forever."

"Just what a wanted to hear!" I hissed back at him, "Thanks for the vote of confidence!" But then, Dad was on to something. I did have a thing for Anna.

Try as I might to stay focused on just getting up to speed on the prime meats industry and Don's companies in particular, I kept losing focus. All I could think about was Anna: her profile, her boldness, her activism, her cool delivery and demeanor. She haunted me. I started to have dreams where she was lying in my arms, and then I'd wake up cold and isolated. I needed to find a way to get to know her without sending her running away.

After syncing up with Don on the details, I got the wild hare to make a trip to NYC by myself, letting Carl know I needed to do an in depth on my own and meet with some of the middle men in the prime meats business, and while I was there, I had to make sure Anna was available to connect with me.

I called Anna by phone with the pretext of business. I got her voice-mail; left a message; heard back from her within a half an hour. This business approach was working. I just had to decide when to confront her about her activism. Now didn't seem to be the right time, and after all, what reason was there to rush it?

"Anna, thanks for returning my call," I said, eagerly engaging with her.

"This isn't Anna," the voice said, "This is Geneviève. What can I do for you?"

"Oh," I was disappointed, "You have Anna's phone?"

"This is her work number for the restaurant. Anna's off this week. She's got business out of town."

"Business?" I asked.

"It's not related to the restaurant. She just said she had something to do. In Chicago."

"Chicago? Is she from there?" I asked.

Geneviève must have realized she was going beyond the scope of what Anna would approve of because she started to hesitate.

"I don't know," she said, tentatively, "I just think she has business there."

There was that word again: business.

"Do you know where in Chicago?" I asked.

Geneviève hesitated. "I know where she's staying, but that's all I know."

"Please give the details. I'll try call her there," I prompted, with no intention of calling at all, but Geneviève didn't need to know that.

She gave me the information.

The next morning, I was on a flight to Chicago. When I arrived, I went directly to her hotel, but she wasn't in the lobby. I had made a reservation to stay there as well, so I left my overnight case with the concierge and took a seat in the lobby. I had to do a bit of detective work to find out what Anna was doing in Chicago. I ran a few internet searches looking for protests or vegan events, but nothing came up. And then I realized that Chicago had been one of main locations for packing plants and slaughter houses, probably the biggest in the US if not the world.

I did a search and found several listings of the biggest meat packing plants and slaughterhouses in Chicago, but they had closed, and the only references I found were related to the CBOT (the Chicago Board of Trade) and the CME (Chicago Mercantile Exchange), both markets for agricultural transactions. There was no way to know what else was going on down there or what business Anna might have there.

I was starting to feel desperate and silly about the whole thing when I overhead a man walking through the lobby ask at the front desk, "Did you see a young woman in a cow outfit?" The man at the front desk shook his head.

That had to be Anna the man was looking for, and I was just about to confront him about it, when I saw a woman get out of the elevator and prance through the lobby dressed as a cow in a costume with large white and black splotches of color on it. She even had plastic udders, a tail, and shoes that looked like hooves. It would have been humorous if it wasn't so hideous.

She walked towards the main door, and the man who had been inquiring about a woman in a cow outfit scrambled after her, saying, "Wait for me! I'm going to film this."

I got up and followed. They walked a short distance to the L train, and I followed them and bought myself a ticket. I had to take a chance that she wouldn't recognize me or that if she did, she wouldn't care that I was following her. She made it easy, dressed conspicuously as a cow. I got on the same train, staying a comfortable distance back so as not to engage with her. Anna had enough of an audience with her fellow passengers eyeballing her that she didn't appear to notice me.

We went some distance, and I exited when she and her companion did. We were in front of a large government building, and as it turned out the CBOT and CME were having a meeting there. Anna and her friend positioned themselves out in front, and as people walked by, she held up a sign that read, "Stop murdering cows", and Anna began making loud mooing noises and also playing the sounds from her recorder. She would walk towards members of the CBOT or CME that she apparently recognized and start contentious rhetoric with them about what they stood for, their lack of responsible action, and their violence towards animals.

The CME was originally known as the Chicago Egg and Butter Board, launching its first futures in the 1960s with frozen pork bellies. Today their involvement was much wider, expanding their trading in forex futures, currencies, stock indexes, interest rate futures, and agricultural products. The CBOT, similarly, established in 1848 as a trading floor for grain merchants in Chicago, was later granted a charter from the state legislature in Illinois and grew into a prominent agricultural futures market. I knew that forex futures are exchange-traded currency derivative contracts obligating the buyer and seller to transact at a set price and predetermined time, and apparently today was when a large meeting of the players of these two boards was taking place, giving Anna and the other animal rights protesters a wider audience, and perhaps the ability to enact change at a deeper level.

Anna continued to accost attendees of this event in her cow costume, making loud mooing noises, and running her recorder's speaker as loud as it would go, as her accomplice followed her and photographed the scene. What was he going to do with the pictures and videos? I could only guess, and in this case, Anna was not nearly as recognizable as she had been at the outdoor event in San Francisco or the restaurant where she had smeared herself in blood and been arrested. At least she couldn't easily be identified by these photos. She just looked like a human dressed as a cow.

I found a concrete ledge by the outdoor vegetation to rest on, and I stayed for the duration of her protesting. She wasn't the only one. There were several people carrying signs and chanting, but Anna was the only one in a bovine costume. As odd as it was from my perspective, I wanted to know more. I wanted to get to know this woman who was willing to do something insidious in many people's eyes; that is, disrupt businesses who disagreed with her with only the threat of violence and embarrassment as her weapons, using her own body and reputation as the spoils to make her point. What motivated her? Why this and not something else? Why the double persona with her role as a manager of a steakhouse in NYC? What was the connection?

She managed to make her way inside the government building, perhaps because the protest was peaceful. No one stopped her, and she and the other protesters disappeared inside. I made my way towards her, but I was stopped at the door and asked what business I had there.

At that point, I realized she had done something different from just attempting to walk in. Somehow, she was allowed in. Who was she affiliated with and how did she manage to get past the guards?

I wasn't giving up. I waited outside, and eventually everyone started leaving the building, but by this time, my enchantment with Anna and her vegan protesting buddies was growing thin. I wanted answers, and I was frustrated, tired, and spent.

Instead of going back to the hotel, Anna emerged with a bag holding her cow outfit inside, dressed in street clothes, and she and her photographer made their way to a vegan restaurant, again by taking the L train. I followed them, and I entered the restaurant when they did. At this point, I felt entitled to something. I wanted answers, and I was tired of the torture of Anna. The idea of her, the smell of her, the strength of her, the conviction of her, the audacity of her: I wanted to know more.

Anna and her escort got a table and were looking at a menu when I approached them.

"May I join you?" I asked.

Anna didn't look away from her menu, but her escort did.

"I don't see why not," he said.

I reached out to shake his hand, as much to find out what his name was if nothing else, "I'm Dan," I said succinctly and supplied no more information.

"I'm Todd," the photographer greeted and went quiet himself.

Anna continued to read the menu, not even flinching or making eye contact with me.

I asked the waiter for a menu and perused the options of macaroni and "vegan" cheese, veggie platters, sugar snap peas and carrot soba noodles, kale, black bean and avocado burrito bowl, and creamy butternut squash ravioli. It didn't sound half bad, and I ordered the squash ravioli for the second time in my life.

Eventually the silence got to me, and I said to Anna, "You're an interesting woman."

She remarked, "So that's what brings you to Chicago. You're following me."

I realized it was true, but I wasn't proud of it. I didn't want to be viewed as a stalker, but I was attracted, drawn to her, obsessed.

I turned to Todd to break the tension, "So what do you plan to do with the photos and videos you took?" I asked.

"Post them," he replied, "to social media. For awareness."

That made sense, and he made it sound so logical. So why did I feel knotted inside?

"You must be wondering," Anna said, breaking the awkward silence, "Why I advocate for the animals yet work at a steakhouse?"

"It did cross my mind," I replied in my normal style of understatement.

"It serves my purpose," she stated simply, "That's all I can tell you."

"Or that's all you **will** tell me," I rephrased her response.

Silence.

"Anna is a complicated woman with a purpose," Todd attempted to clarify, "That's true if nothing else."

"I suppose I am complicated," she agreed, and she ordered from the vegan menu, as did Todd.

"Have you always been vegan?" I asked her.

She smiled, "No, I converted." Still no elaboration, no attempt to figure out what my intentions were. She left well enough alone.

"I see you have," I stated, mimicking the same decisive, deceptive repartee.

"And why do you care?" Anna asked, for the first time showing any attention to me at all. I would have felt flattered if I hadn't been completely at wit's end over her behavior and commentary.

"I don't know," I answered truthfully, shaking my hand, and looking down.

Todd smiled warmly. He had some level of understanding for what I was experiencing.

"Are you wanting to report back to Don about me?" Anna asked.

I didn't know why she asked. I only knew that I would never rat her out.

"No," I answered, "That's not my intention."

"What is your intention?" Anna asked me point blank.

"To get to know you," I said.

"Then you seem to have achieved your purpose. You probably know me better than anyone at this point."

I found myself wondering what that could possibly mean.

Anna smiled at me, and she looked back at Todd, and the two of them had conversation. She asked him how well she had done with making her point; if he thought she had created awareness, raised consciousness around the issues, made any difference at all, and finally she asked him about the photos he took and the videos.

Todd answered all of her questions. He told her how amazed he was at her presence, her steadfast efforts for the animals, and then admitted that he had no idea whether or not she had changed minds or made a difference, but he said he hoped she had. And then he told her the videos and photos would go live in a few days after editing.

Anna seemed satisfied, and Todd excused himself and said good night.

I stayed, and Anna stayed. She hadn't exactly warmed up to me, but she wasn't revolted by me either, and she hadn't publicly rejected me, so I figured that was a win-win.

"Dan," she said, using my name for what felt like the first time, "I'd like to take you with me somewhere tonight. Would you like to go?"

Sight unseen, no questions asked, I just said, "Yes."

SIX

I'll never know for sure what it was: her smile, her confidence, my weakness for attractive women? Perhaps any and all of these things, but I had just agreed to go somewhere in Chicago in the evening with a woman I knew very little about and had good reason to believe might take me somewhere questionable. I was a big boy; I could deal with it. What was life without a little excitement, anyway?

Anna and I took the L train back to our hotel, convenient since I was staying there too, and she put her cow costume back in her room. She asked me to wait in the lobby to go on an "excursion". I could have guessed it might have something to do with her activism. Was she going to introduce me to some people who would try to convince me of something like donating to their cause or giving up meat myself? I couldn't be sure.

When Anna came back, she was dressed in jeans and a jacket with a cap pulled over her ears. She asked me if I was "warm enough", and it wasn't a particularly cold day in Chicago. Yes, it's the windy city, but it was summertime, so I didn't expect it to be cold.

"You might need it," she warned, and I was curious about the alert. I agreed to get my jacket from my room and be right back, which I did in record time.

We set out on the L train again, but this time, I could tell we were going further because she had a map with her and was eyeballing it the whole way. When we did disembark, it was getting dark, and the view was barren. I was surprised she was taking us to a place so far from the city center. I decided to have faith in the process, so I followed her.

She walked at a fast clip looking around as if she had been here before and was trying to see something. Suddenly she identified the landmark she was looking for and signaled to me to follow her, "It's this way." I was surprised she found it at all in the dark, surrounded by buildings that were all similar looking, long and flat and low with a fence encircling them.

Anna led me down a path branching off from the main street, and when we got to the fence, she took the padlock on the gate in one hand, while she used some mysterious looking tool in the other, as she proceeded to pick the lock.

"What's that?" I asked.

"It's a lock picking tool," she responded.

"Obviously," I said, disgruntled, "But why do you have one? Do you do this often?"

"There's a lot you don't know about me," she responded softly, as she let the two of us in, and we walked around the dimly lit facility. I could hear muffled sounds, but it wasn't obvious what I was hearing. She turned on the flashlight from her phone and used it to light our path, suggesting I do the same. We kept moving.

She walked past several of the structures to the back of the enclosed lot, and then she headed for a door where she had to pick another lock.

"How do you know they're not video recording us? Maybe the police are coming?" I asked.

"Not here. I've been here before. It's safe for us," she responded.

Anna opened the door and motioned me to follow her. We crouched down to make it through an entrance with a low ceiling leading into an area that had a slightly musty, stuffy smell. As we proceeded further, there was a light switch, and Anna turned it on.

Immediately noises emanated from the numerous rows of cages in the large open area in the center of the building: squawking, scraping, clucking sounds of birds: large hens. Anna commenced walking through the jail cell layout of cages and again motioned me to follow with her whole arm. As I walked past the door well, I noted a tremendous amount of straw on the floor, and some of it was slippery and patchy. The place stunk with the stench of feces, and it was all I could do to propel myself forward into the vast open space, filled with cages containing hens in close proximity, thrashing around but barely able to do so because they were so large in their mid-bodies. They collided into each other, squawking, ruffling their sparse, patchy feathers, and cocking their beakless heads.

Anna stopped past the first few sections of cages that we walked through, and said to me, "Do you see that their beaks have been removed to prevent them from pecking? It also keeps them from any normal behaviors that chickens do like scratching and cleaning themselves to avoid getting lice. They are in extreme pain after having their beaks seared off with a hot blade, which often harms their nerves, causing them to lose feeling and not be able to consume their feed properly. They feel helpless and become passive, physiologically stressed as they suffer."

As I followed Anna and observed the caged hens, I saw ample evidence that what she was telling me was true. Many of them had bald patches where feathers used to be, and they walked in strange, constricted ways. Anna walked further between the rows upon rows of cages, and then she stopped and said, "Notice that the wire mesh of the floors rubs off their feathers, chafes their skin and cripples them. Their bones are brittle, and they are prone to fractures and feather loss, even osteoporosis. They often have liver rupture and die due to the stress and lack of exercise."

In spite of the horrifically overcrowded and crippling conditions, the evidence of savage practices, and the general disgusting feel of the place, the worst part was the overwhelmingly intense, unrelenting, noxious fumes of filthy fecal matter. I didn't know how much more of it I could take.

After finishing the "tour" of the facility, Anna said, "Let's get out of here. I'll tell you the rest outside."

She didn't have any convincing to do. I was wondering how much longer I could tolerate these conditions, let alone imagine what it was like for the hens who lived here. Once outside, breathing the clean air again, Anna continued to enlighten me.

"There are around 30,000 hens in there," she began, "They're called broilers because they are bred for food, not to deliver eggs. Computers control the heating and ventilating systems and the dispensing of their feed and water, which is medicated with drugs to control parasites and deliver mass doses of antibiotics."

I was getting a really ugly visceral reaction from the pit of my stomach to my head. I didn't have any desire to hear the elaboration, but Anna was relentless with her passion to expose every detail of their abuse.

"These hens experience only artificial light; they are never allowed outside to take in natural sunlight. Since they are broilers, bred for their meat, no one cares about keeping them healthy and happy. Hens that lay eggs will actually lay way fewer eggs because their hormones won't trigger properly without natural sunlight, but that's not an issue here, so the abuse continues. Their units are only cleaned once every two to three weeks, and that's why the whole room reeks of that obnoxious ammonia odor."

I was nauseated. I started to have chest and stomach pain, and I couldn't stand up. I vomited into the grass next to the pavement outside the facility. I had never been in such a vile, troubling, revolting place in my life, and I just wanted to get away.

Anna realized that her tactics had worked: I was repulsed from head to toe. We returned to our hotel in silence and parted ways. I don't even think I said good-bye or good night to her. I didn't think once about my attraction to her. I was drenched in annoyance, disgust, and revulsion. I couldn't get the images, the smells, the panicked sounds, and the oppression out of my mind. I was abhorred by what I had experienced, and it was viscerally real and long-lasting.

When I returned home to Tampa, I realized I had not returned any of the phone calls from Carl, Don or my dad, and there plenty of them. My voicemail was full. I listened to all the messages, dazed and unable to process. I was beginning to think I should keep my distance from Anna. She took me to places I didn't want to go, to see things I didn't want to see or experience. I just wanted normal back.

I called Carl and asked him to meet me for an impromptu over beers at our favorite sports bar. He gladly accepted, and we met up there.

"Where have you been, bro?" Carl started, "Your dad was even calling me asking. You just disappeared right when we're in the heart of things here starting to make progress."

"I know," I said apologetically, "It was just something I had to do."

"Like when you took off for San Francisco? That was pretty erratic too, dude. Do you have a tart on the side we don't know about?"

"I won't even dignify that ..."

"With what? An excuse?" Carl interrupted. I had never seen Carl angry before, but lately I seemed to be getting under his skin, "See, I'm ok with your quirks. I've known you forever, but let's not let your 'activities', whatever they are, ruin this gig for us both. Don has put a lot of faith in us, and we have to deliver."

Carl was spot on. I had started off on the right foot, doing the research, getting our game on, but now I was getting distracted, and I didn't want to tell Carl who the distraction was.

"All right, I'm laser focused now, dude. Bring me up to speed."

"You gotta call Don. He's ready to go to the next level with his prime meats agenda, and he needs you spearheading it. I'm just the numbers guy. You know that."

I did know it, and I was going to do something about it. I called Don an hour later, and we hashed it out over the phone.

"You can't do that to me," Don started, "I need your thumb on the pulse."

"You mean finger," I corrected.

"Huh?" Don sounded irritated, but I had to start getting things right, and that meant getting everything right, even the puny details.

"Your thumb has a pulse, so technically you want me to keep my finger on the pulse, not my thumb."

"Jesus, Dan, you're killing me here," Don fired back. I could see him shaking his head in frustration, "Business details, correct me all you want, but the semantics stuff; just let it go! Pick your battles wisely, kid!"

We were back to him calling me "kid" like when he was referring to Carl and me as "boys" before Anna showed up, and he went to "men". I wanted his respect back. I wanted him to refer to me by name or as a "gentleman" at the very least.

"I'm in, Don. All the way, I want to make this succeed," I verbalized my commitment, and I meant it.

"That's great, Dan. Now prove it! Show me how you can improve profitability in the prime meats business from start to finish by thirty percent. Let's make this happen."

"I'm working on that as we speak," I assured him, and I was. The next day I spent the whole day on the phone with the prime meat providers, the butcher about the cuts, Geneviève about the restaurant in Anna's absence, not even asking for Anna and striving desperately to stay on track to delivering profit for Don and Carl and my dad. I didn't want to disappoint any of them.

"Hey," Dad opened my bedroom door where I was at my desk working on the details, "You ok?"

"Yeah," I assured him too, "I'm good, Dad, just needed a break. I'm back at it."

"I knew you would be!" he sounded as confident in me as ever, "Want to get something to eat? What do you say we go to that new steakhouse and talk prime meats?"

I wanted to let Dad in my world, but after my experience in Chicago, it just wasn't happening for me.

"I can't tonight, Dad, I have plans," I lied outright to my dad for probably the first time ever. My Dad was someone I never had to lie to because he was supportive of me in everything I did. Why was this any different? I couldn't explain it in words, even to myself, but I knew it was decisively different.

That night I tossed and turned and woke up in a sweat, and by morning, I decided I had to call Anna and have the same discussion with her that I was having with everyone else. She was back at work now; there was no reason to avoid her. After all, we worked for the same organization, and I needed to run the show. Avoiding her was not the solution.

Anna set aside some time for us to conference call, and she started off with the proverbial question: "Which came first the chicken or the egg?"

"You got me there," I said, not wanting to waste any time reminiscing or reflecting on the Chicago ordeal, but I did want to solve our business dilemma, "I'm hoping you can help me with something."

She didn't respond, but I knew I had her attention.

"We need to increase profitability in the restaurant, and so far, Don's been fixed on prime meats, but I'm wondering ... is there another way?" I prompted her to go there, to do what my gut told me she was dying to do.

"I like where you're headed with this," the tone of her voice told me she was deeply engaged, "What if we expand our menu to include some foods outside the norm? Some gourmet vegan options? Cauliflower steak extraordinaire? Layered vegetable soufflé? My brilliant ideas just keep coming," Anna said provocatively.

"Yeah, I think I'm on board with this and can potentially bring the players around to it, but I'll tell you truthfully, it's going to be a hard sell. I think you know that."

"So how do we soften it, big boy?" Anna jostled playfully with me, hitting me where I lived.

"We have to bring in the money; it's all about profitability, and people won't pay for vegetables what they will for meat. We need the allure, the sophistication, the attraction, and it has to taste divine, and customers have to be willing to pay for it. Do you think there's a big enough audience for vegan delicacies?" I challenged.

"Do you mean is my life's work real?" she sounded perturbed.

"I mean we have a golden opportunity, but it's not going to do the work itself. People walk away from healthful food; we know that! Not until they are dying of cancer do people take their diet seriously, and fine dining isn't exactly all about the tofu. We can't launch this and have it sink because we didn't do the due diligence to get it right."

She paused, and then she came around, "I'm proud of you, Dan," she said. It was a little demeaning, but I would take it for a lead-in.

"Ok, I'll bite. Why's that?" I asked defiantly.

"The chicken factory really got to you."

She was right. I couldn't deny it.

"So, let's do something about it!" I challenged her again, "Let's make sustainable profit that impresses Don and the rest of NYC."

"I see where you're going with this. All right, I'll start working on it."

And with that, I realized that Anna and I were on the same team. Now I just had to get Carl and Don on that team, and maybe without telling them too much yet. I had to have some way of appeasing them about the prime meats end of things. It was a tall order, but I was up to the task.

There was just something about Anna. I couldn't stop thinking about her.

❦ SEVEN

I decided to find out more about gourmet vegan food. There were a number of locales offering cauliflower steak as an option, but when I called a restaurant that offered it and talked to their management, who to my delight took my call; they said primarily people with serious health issues ordered it; people who'd had a heart attack or a stroke, not ordinary people who were health conscious.

I asked why, sort of "deep down" knowing the reason myself, and the manager said, "No one goes to a steak house looking for cauliflower." That pretty much said it all. While a family might have that "black sheep" relative who refused to eat meat, the main audience, the primary customers of the business, were not vegans, or even vegetarian for that matter, and I found myself contemplating the differences between the two.

Of course, logically a vegetarian doesn't eat meat, but may eat eggs, cheese, and milk, while a vegan doesn't eat or use animal products, forgoing leather for vinyl or another synthetic alternative, but knowing Anna, I realized it went much deeper. Vegans cared about the planet, just like Millennials, and I should know, because I am one. If I were forced to think about how the animals were treated, like I had been when I visited the chicken factory, I couldn't resolve the hypocrisy, and no one wants to be viewed as a hypocrite. I couldn't even live with myself as one.

I made some other inquiries, and I gathered all kinds of information. Indian food was largely vegetarian, especially from the Hindu perspective more so than the Muslim one, although both religions played a large part in Indian culture. Many Americans enjoyed Indian food, but even delicious Indian food was often viewed as an "ethnic" alternative, not a high-end gourmet food commanding a high price. There were other ethnic foods that were primarily vegetarian, like Ethiopian food with its Injera bread, which had this thin spongy consistency, a bread-like product that they could lay down like a pancake on your plate and top with vegetarian purées; of course, pure vegetarian wasn't a requirement; Ethiopians also ate something called "zil zil tibs", which was pure beef. Again, none of these items were considered gourmet, and none of them could command the kind of gourmet pricing Don Price was expecting for the steakhouse, but did it have to be a "steakhouse"?

Was rebranding it – actually gutting the place and recreating it from the ground up an option? Would I have to sell Don and the other players on this, or could I get enough leverage to do it on my own? Maybe I should just lie low and let it roll with high end superior cuts of beef for a while, and in the meantime, figure this all out while gaining a great reputation as a team player who was committed and all in? I still hadn't figured this out. I needed clarity.

I didn't have that luxury. The phone rang. The kitchen was on fire: literally. Geneviève called to inform me that a fire had gotten out of control, and much of the building was destroyed, but fortunately the fire fighters had arrived and put it out. I asked if a report had been filed, but Geneviève was evasive. She said she didn't know. I asked her where Anna was; after all, she was the manager, but Geneviève said she wasn't there, so I asked her what caused the fire, and predictably, she claimed she just didn't know.

It felt too coincidental. I started thinking about Anna in a new way. Yes, I was enchanted with her. There was no other way to put it. I had to admit it. There was something about her that drove me crazy. At the same time, I was responsible for the success of the restaurant and Don's prime meats agenda. I had to do something.

I hopped a flight to New York, and when I arrived, I went directly to the restaurant. Of course, it was late and closed due to the fire, but I called the police, and they agreed to meet with me. I made my way to the station.

The officer in charge invited me to have a seat in a small conference room, and he shut the door. He was a young, fit man, probably in his thirties.

"What caused the fire?" I asked, after showing him my ID and explaining that I was the owner of the restaurant, and I was responsible for its success.

"It looks like tampering," he stated matter-of-factly.

"Tampering?" I asked.

"Foul play," he added.

"You're saying arson?" I exclaimed.

"It's under investigation, and what I can tell you ... Mr. Heller?"

"Call me Dan," I encouraged. I didn't know if it would help, but I wanted him to trust and inform me.

"What I can tell you," the officer reiterated, gathering his train of thought and choosing his words carefully, "is whoever did this intended to start a fire and intended for it to do a lot of damage, even put the restaurant out of business."

"How can you know that?" I shouted, losing my cool.

"Please keep your composure, Mr. Heller," he perpetuated with the formality, "This is a police station. I'm sure you don't want to be restrained."

I didn't, and I realized I was over-reacting. The officer was only going to tell me what he was going to tell me, and there was nothing I could do about it but go along for the ride.

"All right, of course, but since I'm responsible, I want to make sure we find whoever did this. Was there a surveillance video that shows you anything?" I inquired.

"We looked, and it didn't seem to be running."

"You mean the videos were turned off?"

"That's true."

This was a problem. Anna would have had control over the videos. I began to realize that since she was an animal rights activist running a steakhouse, there was definitely a disconnect here that I needed to investigate, and I knew it wasn't going to make her happy, but based on what I knew so far, she was most likely the culprit.

I left the station and found my way to an open café where I called Anna. She answered on the second ring.

"It's Dan," I said, nothing more. I needed to know what she would acknowledge without my probing.

"You must have heard about the fire," she stated.

"Not from you," I accused, "And you are the manager of the restaurant, after all."

"I am, and I will sort this out, but I was sourcing some new products when it happened, so I wasn't on site. I was as shocked as you are."

I didn't confirm or deny my shock, but I did want to meet up in person.

"I'm in town. Can you meet me? I'm at a café having coffee."

"Sure, I'll be right there."

This gave me a reason to believe her. Maybe she would explain something to me because right now the guilty finger was pointing directly at her.

I was munching on a chicken pot pie, no excuses on the meat, when Anna walked in. She didn't disappoint. She never did. She had a tailored, dark colored rain coat on and tall rain boots, which made sense given the recent showers. She looked wind-blown as she walked directly over to my booth and took a seat across from me.

"You flew out here for this?" she said, looking incredulous, as she settled in, collapsed her umbrella, and settled her things around her.

"Of course, I have to get to the bottom of it," I stated simply, noticing that I was tense and must have sent the message that I wasn't pleased and perhaps suspicious of her, but she didn't react.

"Well, I'm sure the police will do what they can," she conjectured.

"They're investigating. Is there anything I should know?" I asked, keeping it open-ended.

"I'm sure there are a lot of things we both would like to know, like how extensive the damage is, how long the restaurant will be closed, and what it will cost to get things back to normal."

"And maybe who caused it?" I asked.

"It may just have been a random grease fire," she speculated.

"It could be. I'm wondering about the surveillance video," I paused, giving her rope to hang herself.

"Was there anything on the video?"

"The officer said it wasn't being used."

"I think it was shut off."

"Really? You're the manager, and you shut the surveillance videos off?" I was panicked and sounding accusatory.

"Not intentionally, I can assure you. We had in a call for someone to take a look at it, but it was upgraded a few weeks ago, and it wasn't working correctly, so you can check. We did put in a trouble call. They just weren't able to fix it yet, so it was turned off," she explained, not even flinching.

This triggered a whole range of suspicions from my perspective. It seemed like a loaded gun.

"So, tell me where I'm wrong," I began, pausing for Anna to order a coffee, and putting my fork down permanently, no longer munching on my pot pie.

"The manager of the steakhouse is a vegan," I began, "She's also an animal rights activist, and a pretty aggressive one who protests in public and even gets arrested for it because she pours animal blood on herself and walks into other steakhouses, accusing people of murdering animals. Am I right so far?" I was shouting. People were turning their heads to look at us.

"They are murdering animals," she commented.

I continued, "This manager of a steak house, I'm assuming, doesn't disclose this to anyone she works for, like Don Price, for example, my boss, that she is an animal rights activist, and she just keeps running the steak house. Am I still on track?"

"I'm not sure how it's my employer's business what I do in my free time," she persists, still without any visible guilt.

"Then, she takes me to a place where hens are made into processed chicken, and deliberately exposes the person overseeing the operation to a disgusting place that might persuade him against serving meat in a steakhouse, and on the same trip, she protests at a meeting of the CBOT and CME in Chicago. You did all this," I accuse to lay a foundation.

Still not rattled but starting to look indignant, Anna says, "At your request. You followed me on my days off."

"Then, not long after having a conversation with me about offering vegan food at the steakhouse, leading me to believe we were on track to working as a team, and I was trusting you," I paused for effect; Anna didn't visibly react, "a suspicious fire breaks out in the steakhouse, so bad it threatens the business' ability to reopen, and not a small fire, a really big one in the most expensive part of the restaurant, doing considerable damage."

"Which one would expect since fires in a restaurant usually happen in the kitchen where the expensive equipment is …"

"And then the police officer tells me he suspects arson," and I make full eye contact.

"And you're accusing me?" she gasps playfully.

"So tell me you didn't do it."

"Look, no one but you thinks I did. You're grasping at straws! There's no evidence I did anything."

"Then tell me you didn't," I insist, making direct eye contact.

"Let me ask you something," she redirects, "Do you seriously think if we start selling vegan food at a prestigious steakhouse in Manhattan that it's suddenly going to fix everything? Do you think the world will be a more humanitarian place? Do you think it will matter one iota to the thousands of animals being slaughtered and disemboweled every day? Do you honestly believe it will change ANYTHING???" She was shouting and rising out of her seat, turning red, clearly a vehement animal rights activist.

"I get it," I responded, "You are an avid animal rights activist. For sure. No question. Here's the problem: you don't get to set fire to a business because it suits your purposes! That's arson, and people go to prison for that."

"Where's the proof, Dan? That's an outlandish accusation with no proof," she stated calmly, her composure fully intact, and I noticed she didn't deny doing it; she just believed no one could prove she did.

I remained silent, and we stared at each other for a while. It was a contest of wills to see who would flinch first, and I didn't want it to be me, but I didn't feel strong enough to be her match. I truly felt her convictions were deeper than mine, and she would never admit to anything no matter what I said. I didn't even know if I expected her to.

"Anna, don't you understand? I trusted you, and I'm in charge of making sure the restaurant is successful. You doing this doesn't just put you in a bad place; it affects me, too. I work for Don; don't you see the dilemma?"

"Are you saying you're torn between doing the right thing for the animals and making money for the restaurant?"

I didn't know if she was just messing with me or if she really didn't get it.

Once again, she redirected the conversation, "Did you book a hotel for the night?"

I hadn't. I had just jumped on a plane without thinking about it in panic mode.

I looked down and shook my head, partly because it was getting late, and I realized I obviously needed a hotel.

"You can stay at my place," Anna invited, "It's the least I can do."

I thought about it for only a moment. I didn't have a place to stay, and I wanted to see what was really going on with Anna. I had to know the truth.

I went home with Anna.

EIGHT

Since Carol, I hadn't dated. I had thought about women. I was a normal twenty-eight-year-old man, but I had felt rejected, and the issues ran deep, and not going out with women kept me in check.

Besides, I had school and life, and living in denial was easier than fixing it.

Until Anna came into my life. I was starting to let my feelings for her escalate, and it was getting out of control. I was losing control. I could be rational about the business, but I couldn't be rational about her. She could pull me in with a wink or a stare or an invitation to her home.

We took the train, meaning the subway for anyone not from NYC, to her apartment. It was on the third floor, and the building wasn't upscale, but everything in NYC is overpriced. We climbed the steps in silence; she unlocked the door; I followed her in.

"Make yourself comfortable," she said and disappeared.

I decided to look around the place. Maybe I was looking for a clue to solve the mystery of why an Animal Rights Activist manages a steakhouse. Maybe I was just a guy infatuated with a girl, but whatever the reason, I snooped. A Siamese cat slithered into the room and started to follow me around. It felt like it was spying on me in an odd way, and then I realized I was over the top: insecure, paranoid, suspicious. I was also dog-tired from the flight, the visit to the burned down restaurant, the meeting with the police officer, and the conversation with Anna, which wasn't exactly pleasant, and now this, whatever this was.

I found myself wondering what I was doing at her apartment and how I was going to get out of this one. I had to rationalize it to myself before I could even consider what I would say to my dad, Don, or Carl. It was making me crazy. I took a seat in her living room. The Siamese cat jumped into my lap. I couldn't tell if it was a "he" or a "she", but it had piercing blue eyes and its effect on me was similar to Anna's: mesmerizing. I couldn't take my eyes off of it, and I couldn't bring myself to fling it onto the floor, so the cat stayed there, in my lap, eyes on me, and I began to drift off.

I awoke to Anna's voice, "Dan ... Dan ... wake up, Dan."

I was still half asleep, but my eyes cracked open, and I was aware of a fuzzy presence.

"Come with me," Anna's voice instructed.

She took my hand, and I followed her into her bedroom, not knowing that was where I was going, and clearly still half asleep.

She motioned to her bed, where the covers were already pulled down, and I crawled in and closed my eyes. I could feel her untying my shoes and slipping them off, and then I felt her body on mine, as she crawled up my legs, and rested on top of me, fully outstretched, climbing up my body until she laid on top of me with her body pressing to mine and her face inches away from mine, both of us fully clothed.

"Dan," she purred, just like her Siamese, and her lips made contact with mine so fleetingly that I wasn't sure that was what I had felt, but it jolted me, and I awakened, fully opening my eyes and staring into Anna's enchanting blue ones. We stayed locked in our mutual gaze without words, and then Anna began to unzip my jacket, unbutton my shirt, lift up my undershirt and touch my chest. Just as I was getting used to her touch, she planted both palms of her hands flush against my nipples and upper chest, just like a cat. She lifted her hands up and slapped them down hard in place a second time, and then a third time, almost as if she was making sure I was completely alert.

The entire time, I held her gaze. Her hands drifted down my chest to my abdomen, and then she loosened my belt, unbuttoned and unzipped my pants, and breaking our gaze slid her body down until her mouth was just above my crotch. She again made constant eye contact with those sparkling translucent blue eyes, as I watched her long red finger nails glide down to the band of my briefs. She slid her fingers in, fluttering them provocatively close to my private parts and began to stroke my genitalia, allowing her fingers to tickle my balls and then glide up the shaft of my penis until the precise moment when she took her full hand and grasped me in my entirety and began to give me a hand job, all the while locking eyes.

I felt my heart race, my knees shake, the back of my neck squeeze, and against my will, I began to tremble, feeling a mixture of extreme pleasure and fear. My mind swirled. Danger sign amidst feelings of arousal, excitement, and anticipation. At some point, my mind relaxed, and I closed my eyes, allowing the sexual feelings to engulf my being, and when the orgasm hit me, I was in ecstasy.

I let out a loud, long release from the back of my throat. It felt like my body was exploding. Was it because of all the tension built up in me? Was it because it had been so long since I'd been with a woman? Was it my intense feelings for Anna?

Before I had time to assess any of it, Anna slipped away. She pulled her body back below my feet to a child's pose yoga position, and then leaped to her feet, just like a feline, and left the room.

My eyes sprung wide open, but I didn't dare move. I lay there with a frenzy of emotions immobilizing me. Then Anna appeared at the door and said, "You take the bed; you can use the bathroom; I'll sleep in the guest room."

She was gone.

I made my way to the restroom, and then suddenly realized my bathroom travel essentials were in the case I had left in her living room. I opened the door and discovered it was dark and lifeless. Anna had already made her way to the guest room. The Siamese cat was sitting on the chair in the living room that I had occupied a short time ago, perched like a bird on the seat, watching me with its sharp, bright blue eyes. Anna's persona and the cat's persona merged for me, and I began to wonder if I was dreaming. I grabbed my bag, headed into the restroom, took a shower, and got ready for bed. I looked at myself in the mirror and just stared at the image. I was beginning to question my own judgment.

Whether it was my exhaustion or the physical release I'd just had with Anna, I fell asleep immediately and dozed right through to morning, waking to a bright stream of sunlight through my window. I got up, shaved, dressed, and opened the bedroom door, my bag packed and ready to fly back to Florida, knowing that I could get a police report and follow up with the restaurant staff by phone.

I hoped to see Anna and talk to her before taking off. While the sexual experience raised a lot of questions, it wasn't what I wanted to ask her about. I needed to know about the fire. Instead of Anna, her Siamese cat greeted me, standing straight up in the same chair, staring at me. I gazed into those bewitching blue eyes, and I looked around for Anna. I called for her. I opened the guest bedroom door, but it was empty; the bed made.

On the kitchen table was a note, "I had to an appointment to get to. Hope you slept well. We'll talk soon. Have a nice flight home!"

And I left her apartment.

NINE

I expected an angry call from Don, but I didn't get one. I figured he was too busy dealing with his other businesses and expecting me to A-Z this, and that's exactly what I planned to do.

When I arrived in Tampa, I kept a low profile. Fortunately for me, Dad was out, and I had the house to myself.

The phone rang, and it was Mom. She was surprised when I answered.

"Dan!" she exclaimed, "It's so good to hear your voice."

"You, too, Mom," I said in a lackluster tone.

"How are you and your dad doing?" she asked.

"We're getting by. Missing your home cooked meals," I said politely, kissing up to Mom was always an effective way of keeping the peace, besides the fact that it was true about her cooking.

"I'm glad to hear that because I'm planning to come to Tampa."

That surprised me.

"To visit us?" I asked.

"To live," she countered.

Now I was shocked. Dad and Mom had parted ways years ago, and Mom had preferred to live out of state, so this change of venue had my suspicions up.

"Why is that, Mom?"

"I miss you both. Do I need a reason?"

I assumed everyone had a reason, but it wasn't my job to enforce that notion, and I had enough on my plate, so I just said, "No, you don't. When will be arriving?"

"End of the week. I'll email you the details. Can you pick me up at the airport?"

That was the least I could do.

I went into my room and shut the door, just to be on the safe side, and I called Anna's cell. She answered on the second ring.

"What's your cat's name?" I asked.

"Cruella," she replied.

"Seriously? The same name as the witch woman in *101 Dalmatians*?"

"Cruella de Vil? Yes, sort of inspired by that; didn't you get along well with her?"

"I got along better with you it seemed."

She didn't reply.

"I'm just trying to put together what happened," I stated honestly, my voice softening with reluctance to confront her.

"You needed to relax," she replied.

That answer made me uncomfortable. Was she trying to say she just gave me a hand job so I could relax? What a good Samaritan that made her. It was also strange. An animals activist, steakhouse manager who gives men she barely knows hand jobs. I was confused.

"I just want to make sure it was consensual, and you didn't feel coerced in any way," I explained, realizing that I was in a leadership position above her being Don's right hand man, and the conflict of interest that posed put me in a vulnerable position.

Anna began to laugh softly, and I felt stupid.

"You could argue I was the one who molested you," she said.

I hadn't thought of it that way, but it was true. I hadn't made a move on her. In fact, I'd nearly been asleep. I wanted to ask her why she did it. Did she find me attractive? Did she just want to pacify me and keep me from going forward with my accusations of arson?

"Look, let's focus on business for now if we can. Will you let me know when you can reopen the restaurant?" I asked with the best of intentions.

"Of course, Dan, you'll receive an email detailing next steps by the end of the day."

There was nothing more to say.

I decided to keep researching the vegan angle on a gourmet restaurant, but the results were mixed. While there was evidence of a growing number of people in the US embracing veganism, it was primarily for health reasons, not to protect the animals, and even true vegans didn't spend the big bucks in gourmet restaurants. There were plenty of pizza houses, Indian restaurants, Ethiopian restaurants, sandwich shops, and grocery stores dedicated to veganism, but high end Vegan houses to rival steakhouses? No evidence of that.

The question was: would turning the steakhouse into a vegan venue be cost effective? Would it boost revenue? Would keeping it a steakhouse and adding vegan entrées be a way in? It was time to talk to Carl.

Carl and I got together at the Sports Bar for a beer.

"Haven't heard much from you, bro. What's going on?"

I didn't reply.

"Have you been boning that Anna chick?"

Guys must just have radar for this stuff, so of course, I had to deny it.

"Of course not. I've been accumulating data on how to raise revenue thirty percent, like Don asked."

"Ok, and?"

"I'm thinking of incorporating gourmet vegan foods," I proposed.

"Let me get this straight. You, Dan, the normal guy, meat eater, wants to convert our new job in NYC working with prime meats and overseeing a steakhouse as our signature first move into a vegetarian place???"

He looked flabbergasted.

"Vegan, not vegetarian," I clarified.

"What's the difference? Even more strict. What's behind this, dude?"

"I've got to find a way to boost revenue thirty percent, and veganism is on the rise."

"You sure it's not you who's on the rise? Isn't that Anna chick a vegetarian? Is she putting pressure on you?" Carl continued his inquisition.

"I told you," I defended my position, "I'm just gathering data to get something in place to grow revenue."

"Then why don't you start with prime meats?"

Carl asked a good question. That was Don's original directive, and he wanted me to talk to a guy named Leo who provided the prime meats we used at the restaurant, and Don was deeply invested in Leo's business, too. In fact, Leo supplied butcher's best to restaurants all over NYC and was expanding into related cities like Boston, Philadelphia, Charlotte and Washington, D.C.

Carl and I had a conference call with Leo and collected info on his business, all the numbers Carl needed for the books and the planning, and we also talked to him about his plan for growth.

Nothing out of the ordinary occurred. We asked lots of questions; he answered predictably with all the meats he provided and how he wanted to leverage the business nationwide, and then I asked him, "What do you think of vegan alternatives?"

"I don't," he responded.

"You don't think it's a good idea to offer them?" I inquired thoughtfully.

"No, I mean I don't think about that at all."

And by his answer, I gathered he didn't want to think about it.

I persisted.

"We're considering offering some high end options with meat substitutes in our NYC restaurant. I'm thinking it could boost business with the new vegan crowd."

"Nobody goes to a steakhouse to get a broccoli taco."

Carl chuckled. He wanted to tell me, "I told you so," but he held his tongue.

"However," I came back once again, "Some of these meat lovers have dining partners who don't eat meat, and we're losing that segment of the dining market. If we offer vegan options, we can expand our clientele."

"You do that, then," Leo said, unconvinced.

I let it go.

When I picked up Mom at the airport, she could tell something was wrong.

"Are you ok, baby boy?" she asked, tickling me under the chin as we walked to my car.

"I am. I've got a new job that takes me to NYC, and I'm working pretty hard these days."

"Just like your father," Mom replied, "Do you have a girlfriend?"

I shook my head.

"Carol really did a number on you," she commented.

"Mom let's not relive that," I pushed back.

"Nothing about reliving, Dan. You have to move on. You can't let one bad experience ruin your life."

"It wasn't a "bad experience", Mom. I loved Carol, and I wasn't good enough for her. End of story. I'm just not up to going out there and getting beat up all over again."

"Spending your life alone isn't a good option," Mom pointed out, "You have to get back in the game. I want a grandchild!"

Leave it to Mom to turn our first conversation in person in months into a guilt trip.

"I love you, Mom," I assured her, "but I don't want to discuss my love life, or lack thereof, with you. Can we talk about something else?"

"Of course," she said emphatically, "I have some exciting news!"

I was afraid to ask, but I didn't have to.

"I'm starting a cooking school!"

"A cooking school? Here in Tampa?"

It shouldn't have been a surprise. Mom was a great cook, but why a school?

"You remember Roberta Sanders, my good friend of many years; you went to grade school with her daughter ..."

"Yes, Mom," I cut her off, wanting her to cut to the chase, "I remember her."

"Well, she is starting a cooking school in several different cities, and Tampa is one, and she recruited me, so I figured I'd come back to live with you and your dad and cook for both of you; you are looking a bit slim," she said, squeezing my side.

I avoided telling her that I wasn't eating because I was chasing an Animal Rights Activist / Steakhouse Manager / hand job giver around and not getting any sleep.

"And also help Roberta, and give myself something meaningful to do. I'm excited about it!" she smiled.

I thought about it for a moment, and then I said, "You know, Mom, you could be very helpful to me."

Mom shot me a quizzical look.

"What do you know about Vegan gourmet food?"

TEN

Mom was amazing, and that's an understatement. It made me think that maybe I have trouble dating because I'm comparing every woman I meet to Mom. Although, Dad probably won't second that motion, so I guess I should just settle for realizing that Mom delivers in spades.

The day after Mom arrived, she invited me to go with her to meet with Roberta at the kitchen where they planned to offer classes, turning the place into a school. We actually met at what Mom said Roberta referred to as a "dark" kitchen. That alone was mysterious. It turned to be a facility where a professional cook or chef can prepare food for customers without a dining area, so no restaurant facility. It's basically a commercial kitchen, but you can share the building space with other food services that have their own kitchens, saving you money. Most businesses appeared to be using their kitchens to create food for sale on delivery platforms "to go", but Roberta and Mom? They negotiated a deal where students could come to this place and learn to cook from them, and then apparently, they could also sell the food at some point if it went that direction.

"Question," I said to Roberta shortly after we had arrived and she had taken us on a short tour, "do you have plans to make vegan food?"

She smiled, "You must have read my mind," she said, "We are planning to focus on two groups of students," and then she stopped, looked around, and said, "Let's have a seat. I have some things to offer you."

Roberta and her daughter, Evelyn, more informally known as "Eve", had been preparing some dishes before we arrived, and her daughter, clad in an upscale, fashionable no-nonsense apron of a sort with a tall chef's hat, whirled around revealing a tray of appetizers. I also couldn't help but notice that Eve was beautiful. She had high arched eyebrows, and soft, hazel, wide open eyes with those big fake eyelashes all the women are wearing, but somehow, they looked natural on her. She smiled widely and said, "Please, have a seat, and you can try some of these."

There was a table in front of the "dark" kitchen space Roberta had rented where plates, silverware, and napkins were already available, and as Mom and I sat down, Roberta plopped down an appetizer tray in from of us. It was laden with sliders, veggie burgers inside, some Moroccan chick pea medley in little bowls, tzatziki with brown rice crackers, and small veggie pizza tarts on gluten free crusts. She served us hot tea to drink, and we began to taste the items, noting they were all vegan.

Roberta pulled up a seat beside us and said, "One of the groups of students is from a new vegan cruise line. They'll be training to be cooks on these ships. The other group we're preparing to sign a contract with are young chefs who are subsidized by their colleges, and it makes sense to train them in the latest vegan marvels, so that's what we'll be doing. At least, that's what I hoped we'd be doing, and that's why I reached out to your mom."

Roberta looked at mom.

"That's right. For the last few years, I've been focusing on eating clean for all kinds of reasons, but mostly for health and disease prevention. I've developed a lot of my own recipes, and you know I always used to cook for large groups of people," Mom reminded me.

"What do you mean by "clean", Mom?" I asked.

"Clean cuisine is eating simple, whole foods without artificial ingredients," she clarified. It was true. Mom had always been known as a chef, but she had given up her career for my dad before I was born, and then after I was born, she hadn't gone back to work formally, but she had cooked for all dad's dinner parties, wining and dining executives and business targets for as long as I could remember.

"Your mom is so creative and such a great cook, I wanted to get her on board with all of this!" Roberta declared with a large smile on her face, "and here she is!"

We lifted our teas and clinked cups as if they were champagne glasses.

Eve sat quietly at the end of the table.

"What do you make of this?" I asked her.

She smiled tentatively at me, potentially picking up on my attraction for her, although I thought I was hiding it well. It may have been that she was so gorgeous every man was suspect.

"I'm enthralled," she admitted, "I love to cook, and I think this is a great opportunity for us to put a suite of classes together and roll them out to these two groups of students."

As a businessman, I realized it made a lot of sense. They would have contracts; they wouldn't have all their eggs in one basket because there were two disparate groups to service, and they had a "dark" kitchen so expenses would be affordable. It was a win-win.

"I love the idea, and you are all perfect for it. I have an added interest in this," I admitted, "but Mom," I made direct eye contact, "No mention of this to Dad yet — I mean it!"

Mom smiled tactfully, "You should know I never tell your father anything anymore." She sipped her tea thoughtfully.

"All right then, between just the four of us," the ladies drew near me, "I just completed my MBA and Dad referred me to his buddy who runs a Private Equity firm in NYC, and some of his companies are in the gourmet food business," I hesitated, not mentioning prime meats, "and one of the primary businesses he wants me to focus on is a restaurant in NYC, and I have a strong interest in introducing vegan menu items."

Roberta raised her eyebrows as high as her daughters, "Fabulous! You're among friends, and we can definitely work together on this."

Eve shyly looked away, but I caught her eye later in the conversation and picked up on the attraction being mutual.

Nevertheless, I parted ways with the gals under the guise of "getting back to work" so I could return the phone message I had received from the New York police department about the restaurant fire.

I was transferred to the detective on the case, and he told me, "We can't prove arson."

"Excuse me?" I questioned him, "I thought you guys were sure there was foul play."

"We saw the signs, but the video footage is missing, and we don't have any witnesses. It looks like your insurance will be able to cite reference to suspected arson, but there won't be any arrests."

I was disappointed, but in a way, it worked better this way. I wouldn't have to confront or fire Anna. Instead, I called Don. Fortunately for me, he hadn't been informed of the fire.

"Don, I have bad news, but I'm on top of it."

"What's that?" he sounded panicked.

"There was a fire at the steak house in NYC."

"Good God; how much did we lose?"

"There was damage. I saw it. I flew out there and met with the police, and I just got off the phone with the detective in charge."

"Excellent! Great to know you're on top of things. Give me a full report."

"The insurance should cover it; arson was suspected, but they couldn't prove it. Somehow the surveillance video equipment wasn't operational, and I'm going to get on that right away, and I'll oversee the rebuild and get us back in business. I'll have to get back to you on just how long we'll be closed, but I'll see if I can speed things up, and plan some type of a big re opening to get business back on track and moving towards that thirty percent increase you expect."

"You're the man," Don praised me emphatically.

I had a plan, and I was going to execute it. It didn't matter whether or not Anna was on board. If she wasn't, I would fire her and make progress anyway. The vegan idea that I wouldn't have encountered without her was still the best idea to grow the business the thirty percent in revenue Don expected, and as long as we kept prime meats moving at the same time, I couldn't imagine Don would have a problem with it. It was my job to make sure that happened.

I called Anna, got her voicemail and left a message: "You're off the hook this time, but I expect video surveillance working by my next surprise visit to your restaurant, and you just never know when that's gonna be, so ASAP! Get on it!"

I liked the authority I heard in my voice. Next, I called Mom's cell.

"Hey, hon. I thought you were working. Is everything ok?"

"Yes, are you still at the dark kitchen?"

"I am. Here with Roberta and Eve."

"Can you give me Eve's cell number?"

I could see Mom's smile in my vivid imagination as she said, "Of course, I can."

We hung up, and I called Eve.

"Hi," she sounded self-conscious. I imagined her in front of my mom and hers.

"Are you busy tonight? I was thinking we could have dinner," I suggested.

"I'd love to," she said without a second's hesitation.

I spent the rest of the afternoon actually working. For some reason, my mind was free, and I touched base with Leo and arranged to get prime meats distribution moving in various locales, went over Carl's numbers and gave him feedback, updating all the players on our projections, and set the wheels in motion to get vegan food items on our NYC menu, and then I got ready for dinner with Eve.

Eve and I met at an Italian restaurant we both knew in Tampa. I suggested Italian because I knew they'd have both vegan and non-vegan entrées. I arrived a few minutes early and got us a table.

Eve walked in dressed in a leopard bodycon that eliminated the possibility that she wasn't attracted to me. Her attire and her look told me everything I needed to know, but she still seemed timid, unsure of herself, walking in discreetly looking down.

I made every effort to boost her ego.

"You look amazing!"

She smiled and looked up at me, and I jumped out of my chair, pulling hers out for her like a gentleman. She eagerly took a seat and scooted up to the table, dragging the bottom of the chair, springing forward in her spiked heels like a leopardess on the hunt.

I kept the conversation light. Eve was predictable. She had lived in Tampa with her parents her whole life. Her grandparents on her father's side came from Cuba, and she had lovely tanned skin. She was soft spoken and laughed easily. She loved to cook; she liked Italian food.

I found my mind wandering to Anna, and it bothered me. I saw images of Anna in my mind's eye, and I tried desperately to stop them.

Eve asked me if I had a girlfriend.

"No," I answered, "I dated a woman named Carol for like five years, and no one since then."

She looked uncomfortable.

"Why did you drop her?" she asked, looking fearful.

"I didn't. If anything, she dropped me." I didn't want to explain.

"Ok," Eve smiled quietly, and we went back to meaningless conversation about the food, her job and mine, and the night life in Tampa, and gradually it became a formula. I knew what to do, what to say, and I would do it, but I wasn't intrigued by her. I couldn't stop fantasizing about Anna.

After dinner, I asked Eve back to my place. I had my own room, and we could go in through the back entrance, so even if Mom was home, she wouldn't see us, and Dad never butted in my affairs.

"Ok," Eve said, agreeing in a non-committal way, but my intentions had been clear. She knew why I was asking her back to my place.

She followed me in her car and parked on the street, accompanying me inside. I offered her a seat in the chair at my desk while I sat on the bed. I made stilted conversation with her for a few minutes, and then I realized I was never going to get past Anna if I didn't make a play for

Eve. The brief instance of intimacy in Anna's apartment where she gave me a hand job had reawakened my sexuality, and I wanted more.

I moved towards Eve and put my hand on her leg. She looked uncomfortable, but I continued to pursue her. I stroked her leg, looked into her eyes, and she responded. I pulled her towards me, and she left the chair, gliding towards me onto the bed so that we were lying side by side. I began to grope her with abandon, first circling her areola outside the leopard print top with my fingers, and then cupping her breasts with my hands, squeezing them gently and then more vigorously. She allowed me to do this, but I didn't get the feeling she was fully engaged. She seemed to be holding back, so I said, "You have beautiful breasts," and she relaxed a bit. She seemed to need reassurance every step of the way.

I slid my hands to her waist and poked through the leopard print material to her belly button and pressed on it, tickling her playfully, and she laughed. Then I moved my hand down to the crotch, lifted the hem of her bodycon, and fingered her panties. I took my fingers inside her panties, gently probing the lips of her labia and inviting them to open, and when they did, I began to stroke the sides, careful not to fully plant my finger on her clitoris. She began to writhe a bit and moan. I was in.

Just to be on the safe side, I added the reassurance she craved, "You feel fantastic," I said.

She loosened up and began to move more. I pressed my index finger firmly on her clit and began to make same circular motions with careful, variable pressure. She started to moan louder, and she said, "Oh, God, it feels so good."

"Let me get a rubber," I said, moving away from her and heading to my bathroom, hoping I even had one, it had been so long since I'd be sexually active. I found it, and when I returned, she had removed her leopard dress and was lying there in a lacy bra with her panties still on. She obviously wanted me to take them off.

I set the rubber to the side, still fully dressed, and I lowered my mouth to her panties. I slid my fingers inside and began to rub her again; she was sopping wet and moaning. I slid my tongue inside her panties and began to stroke her clit with swift movements from side to side and then around, and each time I went around she moaned loudly and repeated, "Oh, God!" I slipped off her panties and tossed them to the side, took off my belt, unbuttoned my fly and unzipped my pants; I put the rubber on and held her arms to the sides, realizing I was fully hard, my mind obsessing with images of Anna. I shoved my member into her vagina with some fervor, and she gasped. Eve went slightly limp and seemed less engaged, but I didn't waver. I began to pump her, shoving myself into her again and again with vigor and ferocity. She whimpered softly, no longer moaning, but I barely took note; I was fueled on by my desire to rid myself of the conflict. There was a relentless, driving force in my body, my heart, my mind that I wanted to conquer my desires. I desperately needed to prove I didn't need Anna. I didn't want Anna. I was a man of passion and desires that Anna had awakened in me, but I didn't need her. I could fuck Eve, and I did. I came hard.

It felt a bit awkward afterwards. I immediately got up and went to the bathroom to dispose of the rubber and clean myself, but I ran warm water on a towel and took it back to Eve, saying, "Here, this will help you clean up."

She said nothing, but she took the towel, and I returned to the bathroom, zipped up and put my belt back on and waited while Anna redressed in her leopard outfit. Her makeup was smeared all over her face when I re-entered my room, and I asked her, "Do you want anything before you go?"

She shook her head "no" and said nothing. I opened the door and said, "Have a nice night," and she left.

I went to bed, but I felt miserable. I couldn't believe I had done what I had, but in one way, I didn't regret it. For so long I had felt bad about myself, like no woman would be interested in me since my breakup with Carol, and now I didn't feel that way anymore.

I was concerned Eve might say something to her mother or mine or both, and that wouldn't be good for me and the business. I needed

my mom's help with the vegan agenda, but I figured she wouldn't abandon me over this. She might be angry or disappointed, depending on
what Eve said, but then Eve had willingly come to my room after dinner
dressed in a leopard bodycon. She had given her consent to have sex
with me. I had aroused her with my mouth and my touch before having
sex with her, but then I hadn't really given a damn about her. I had no
interest in dating her. I didn't even like her. I didn't care that she hadn't
come and didn't even really think about it. I had obviously been overcome with lust and passion to prove something that had nothing to do
with Eve and everything to do with my relationship with Anna. I wasn't
sure how to come to terms with that.

I decided to leave it for another day, and I went to sleep.

ELEVEN

I decided it was time for my "surprise visit" to NYC to make sure the surveillance videos were working, among other things. I told myself I could visit Leo and have a chat about prime meats and also eat at the steakhouse and further perfect the menu, but realistically, I just wanted to see Anna.

I was seated in the restaurant early, around 4:45 pm, just before opening, sampling some of the meats with Geneviève, when Anna arrived. She wasn't alone. There was a tall, dark haired, brown-skinned man with her wearing a fashionable suit, walking in hand in hand with her, as they swung their arms comfortably back and forth. She was giggling softly, seeming much less hard, strong, confident and more vulnerable, sweet, and innocent than before. It engaged me.

They meandered over to our table, and Anna introduced him to me, "Raj, this is Dan; Dan, this is Raj", and before I could say anything, as I was in the process of pushing chair back and standing up to shake his hand, she said, "My fiancé."

I felt my heart drop to my knees, and I was speechless. I could barely stand. Why was she having this kind of effect on me?

"Raj," she said playfully, "This is my boss, Dan. He oversees the place from Tampa."

Raj had bright dark eyes, and he looked me square in the face, and said, "Nice to meet you," shaking my hand aggressively. I noted an Indian accent if I wasn't mistaken.

I returned the pleasantry, but my confidence was shaken, and I struggled to preserve my composure.

"Raj ..." I began, "You're a lucky man."

It was truthful. It was all I could manage. Anna shot me a surprised glance with one lifted eyebrow.

"I know it," he agreed, "Anna is quite the woman."

"Speaking of that," I said, recovering, "She's also quite a manager, and I'm wondering, Anna, can we talk about the restaurant tonight? I have a few important questions for you."

"I didn't know you were coming," Anna said with intention, making a point of my reference to a "surprise" visit as leaving me open to coming at the wrong time, "Otherwise, I wouldn't have invited Raj to come with me tonight."

"Nonsense!" Raj chimed in too quickly, "I have no problem with it. This is your boss, so of course you should meet with him since he flew in from Tampa today. I'll get a table, order, and wait for you! Why don't you two talk now and then you can join me?"

Anna smiled warmly at him, "You're always so accommodating. I love you so much," she announced publicly in a way I felt was unnecessary.

Raj left with Geneviève, leading him to an open table, and Anna sat down across from me, softly, slowly, and with total control. She was always one step ahead of me.

"The video surveillance equipment ..." I began.

"Is working," she finished my sentence, "Someone on staff can show you. I'm off tonight, and Raj and I are having dinner date."

She was deliberately pushing my buttons now.

"I'm glad it's working. Thank you for doing as I asked."

"Well, it's the least I could do since you accused me of being an arsonist in the restaurant I manage," she smiled slyly. No shame.

My emotions were raging out of control. I could feel my heart beating rapidly; I was so attracted to her. My eyes noted her cleavage peeking out of her polished satin blouse in lavender and her long purple fingernails. I remembered those nails touching my private parts just a week earlier, and shivers of excitement went up my spine.

We were alone at the table, and Raj had granted us a meeting, so I figured I might as well take advantage of the opportunity.

"You look ravishing," I began. I couldn't help myself. It was true. I didn't concern myself with how she would react.

She laughed, "Yes, I can see how you would see it that way."

"What does that mean?" I snapped back defensively.

"Well, just because I gave you a hand job doesn't mean I'm into you. In fact, now that you've met my fiancé, who I'm in love with, by the way, that's been made completely obvious."

I felt duped, tricked, undermined, but I couldn't fathom why. I couldn't make sense of my own reaction, and it troubled me.

"I need your help with the vegan menu items," I said, changing the subject to regain my composure.

"Of course, I can do that," she replied.

I was silent. What else could I say?

She looked ready to leave, but before she could move her chair back in anticipation of heading over to Raj, I said, "How is Cruella?"

"My cat?" she laughed.

"Yes, your cat."

"She's feeling frisky. I think I need to find her a mate."

There was an awkward silence between us.

Geneviève returned, and Anna asked her to work with me on the vegan items and also demonstrate that the video surveillance equipment was now working, and she left. Anna seductively strutted over to Raj's table, and she snuggled up next to him, touched his arm lovingly, patted it repeatedly, threw her head back spontaneously and let out a long, free, charismatic laugh. I was enraged.

The confidence I had achieved by having sex with Eve was short lived. I now felt jilted. I decided to stay in NYC for a while. Dad owned an apartment there, and the tenant had recently moved out, so I moved in. Conveniently, it was near Anna's place. After dining at the steakhouse, I stayed a bit longer to do some work on the financials and make sure I was up to speed. I took the office in the back to work privately, and at the end of the evening, I heard some noise and ventured out to see who was still there.

It was Anna.

"I thought you had gone home with Raj," I commented.

"He has to work in the morning," she replied with no further embellishment.

"So you didn't go home with him?" I asked.

"We don't live together," she explained.

I found that odd.

"I'm staying at an apartment my dad and I own in the city. It's pretty big and furnished, and the tenant just moved out, so I'll be here for a while. We can meet up tomorrow if you like."

"Why don't you take me there tonight and show it to me?" Anna asked directly.

It was forward. It was strong. I was titillated to the extreme.

"I'd like that," I said softly.

Anna and I took the train and walked together to my building in silence. There was an unspeakable energy between us that I found perplexing. I felt connected to her without talking, sharing, or discussing anything. The connection was visceral, deep, sharp.

I opened the door, and she entered in lock step with me.

"I'm surprised Raj doesn't mind that you are visiting other men at night," I remarked.

"I do as I please," she commented, and she looked around the place; I could tell she was impressed. Dad had decked the apartment out for client meetings or extended stays in the city; he used to bring me here on vacation with Mom, and she had decorated it to be a second home for us.

"This is lovely," she said, sweeping her hand across a table top.

"It works for us," I commented, "Can I get you a drink?"

I made my way to the bar where I poured myself a scotch.

"I'll have one of those," she said.

I found it odd that she was following my lead. She usually set the stage, disagreed with me, created tension, but tonight was unusual. She was in sync with me. Why was this happening? I decided to ride it out and let it happen.

"Of course," I said, grabbing a second cocktail glass, pouring twice, and handing her one. We sat together in the living room.

I saw this as my opportunity to get to know Anna better, so I went for it.

"I find you fascinating," I admitted honestly, "How do you reconcile being an animal activist and a steakhouse manager?"

"Here we go again," she said, stifling a belly laugh, "Things aren't always what they seem."

It was a strange reply. I didn't know what to make of it.

"Why did you come here with me tonight?" I asked, staying direct but changing course on topic.

"I like that question better," she responded provocatively, "I think you and I have something in common."

I liked where this conversation was going.

"What's that?" I asked naively.

She pulled her head back, eyes to the ceiling in a full body laugh, "Oh, Dan," she said, "Do I have to say it? You and I both like to fuck."

I shouldn't have been shocked, but I was. I said nothing, but I turned beet red.

Anna set her drink down and walked over to me. She bent down in front of me in a crouching position and placed both hands on my thighs.

"Shall we go to the bedroom?" she asked.

I didn't have to be asked twice.

The bed was a waterbed, the old fashioned kind with the big waving mattress that my parents had moved in years ago. I loved it. It was like swimming and sleeping in the ocean.

"Oh, the waves!" Anna remarked with delight.

It was also decked out with golden satin sheets. Perfect for our first full body encounter.

"I'm going to slip into something more comfortable," Anna said, retreating to the bathroom, "Why don't you jump into bed and get ready for me," she invited in a sultry tone.

My heart was pounding, and I was fully aroused. I had never been with a woman whose voice alone could send me over the top. I was losing control. I made my way to the bed, turned down the covers, and removed my shoes, socks, pants and shirt but left on my briefs. I slid under the covers and propped myself up onto my forearms with a full view of the exit from the bathroom. I turned on the music in the bedroom, and a romantic, erotic African rhythm filled the room.

Anna emerged minutes later in a tasteful, simple negligee, all in black. She was wearing a satin robe, open in front and loosely fitted around her shoulders that she kept on all the way to the bedside, moving like a panther in fluid, long steps. She stopped within full view of me on my side of the bed and let the robe float to the floor, revealing her shapely, toned, firm body in the

black silk of the negligee, and she just stood there for what felt like an eternity, making deep eye contact with me.

I felt I was going to jump out of my skin. I didn't care any more about the possibility that she had set fire to the restaurant. I didn't care that it didn't make sense that she was an animal rights activist managing a steakhouse. It didn't matter that she couldn't answer a direct question about anything. I could have cared less that she was willing to taunt me and embarrass me in front of others. Nothing mattered except being with her; being possessed by her: emotionally, physically, completely.

Anna stepped towards me, and I trembled. She climbed on top of the bed and made her way towards me like a feline, slithering through the sheets on all fours and landing at my side, watching me with no physical contact. I was comfortable letting her call all the shots. I didn't move.

She smiled seductively. "I want you," she said without doing anything. I replied, "I want you, too."

"I want you to touch me," she said.

I lifted my hand, but she shook her head.

"I want you to do what I tell you to do."

I smiled, "Of course."

"Run your hand down my leg."

That was easy enough. I did it.

"Slowly," she instructed.

I complied.

"I like that," she confirmed, "Now squeeze my ass."

I did.

"Harder, really grasp it in your hand; use both hands; both cheeks."

I did as she demanded.

She smiled again.

"Now move your hands up the backs of legs towards my buttocks and circle back and up, ending with the buttocks squeeze."

I hesitated, focusing on what she was saying.

"Do it, now!" she commanded.

I did it.

"Now touch yourself."

I lay there waiting for instruction.

"Good," she said, approving of the full control she had over me.

"Pull out your cock," she instructed, as I lay there in only my briefs.

I did as she said.

"Masturbate yourself," she commanded.

I gave myself a hand job, watching her the whole while. It was a tantalizing experience, and I felt myself coming to a climax much too soon.

"Stop!" she commanded.

I did.

She jumped on top of me, firmly planted me at the entrance of her vagina, and descended upon me. I was not wearing a condom, and I didn't care. She took all of me, stuffing the fullness of my member inside of her, and she sat on me. She began making small circles to the right and the left, slowly, as she threw her head back and raised her eyes to the ceiling. It was unbearable. I held off as long as I could, but I could no longer control myself, and I came. Afterwards, I passed out from the intensity.

When I awakened, she was gone. I cleaned myself off and went back to bed. I fell asleep, at peace with the world.

Twelve

When I awoke in the NYC apartment, I wasn't nearly as elated as I had been the night before. In fact, I was deeply troubled. Nothing was going the way I wanted it to. I wanted a relationship with Anna, and all I had was a strange control freak manipulating me. I wanted to be successful in business, and I was grasping at straws with it, alienating the people I needed most. Carl and I were at odds; my mother was starting a business with a woman whose daughter I had used for sex, and my relationship with Don wasn't completely truthful. I knew I was in trouble, I just had no idea what to do about it.

I flew back to Tampa the next day hoping to make things right. Mom had left a note on the kitchen table, "Meet us at the dark kitchen."

Here we go again, I thought, only this time Eve wasn't likely to be so happy to see me. I decided to take it like a man, and I went to the kitchen. When I arrived, it was much more lively than the first time I had visited; there were lots of people using various kitchens in the building, and there was a lot of noise, delicious smells and activity, people scurrying around, laughing,

chatting, and having what appeared to be a great time.

I headed over to Mom's area, and I was pleased to find her and Roberta cooking up a storm. "Join us," Roberta shouted, motioning me over, "We have some delicious vegan foods for you to try and recipes galore!" She pushed a plate towards me. Just as I was getting settled and starting to feel comfortable, Eve walked in. She had a plastic smile on her lips. Both of our moms greeted her fondly, and it was obvious she hadn't mentioned our encounter to them. I was grateful. Maybe she was ok with my mistake?

I greeted her, "Hey, Eve."

"Hey yourself," she said, and hurried over to her mom's side to start working on the recipes they were preparing. I also felt disrespected, but I realized my expectation was unreasonable. She didn't owe me anything, and I was the one who had treated her like a piece of meat. She had every right to treat me the way she was.

Roberta finished putting the final touches on a sugarless flan that she passed around the table, and then she invited all of us to sit for an update.

"Exciting news! We signed our first contract!" she was beaming, "We open in three weeks, and in the meantime, Eve is going to spearhead our vegan menu, so Dan, she'll be working with you!" Roberta shot a look to my mom that she reciprocated. I knew when I was getting set up.

I went to say something, although I don't know what it would have been, but Eve beat me to it, "I don't know, Mom. I don't want to restrict myself to vegan food. I could do a great meat lineup."

Roberta looked disappointed, "Meat dishes are fine, but we need veganism for the cruise ship line, and the college kids are expecting that too since we pitched it to their decision makers, so we have to do that for now."

I got the sense Eve just didn't want to work with me and her protest was her lame attempt of getting out of it. I could do better.

"Actually, the restaurant in NYC is a steakhouse in bed with prime meats, so it doesn't look like we'll be going vegan anytime soon. Sadly," I admitted looking around at all three women to show my truthful intentions, "I was looking forward to working with all of you, but it looks like I jumped the gun. I can't do it right now."

Before my mom could jump in and back Roberta up to insist, Eve jumped in and said, "Great because I'm pretty busy, too."

"All right," Roberta sighed, "For now, let's just enjoy the food!"

She passed around an array of vegan delights, and we all shared them. Afterwards, I decided to confront Eve, but I wasn't sure how best to do it.

"Eve, can we talk?" I decided to be direct.

She looked away but grudgingly agreed with an unenthusiastic nod.

"Do you mind if we grab a cup of Joe?"

She reluctantly went along with me, but I could tell she'd prefer to be anywhere else. Our moms smiled at us knowingly, assuming we were getting along romantically, but we both knew differently.

We chatted about the new contract and the food on the way to get coffee, and once we arrived, I ordered us a couple of lattes, and then we sat at a table. Eve's eyes were staring at the floor. It was time for me to nip this in the bud.

"I'm sorry. Truly, I am. I didn't treat you well the night we went out."

Eve said nothing initially, and then grudgingly she said, "I thought you just wanted me for sex."

"I find you very attractive," I admitted, "And I enjoyed our time together, but since my breakup with Carol, I haven't been myself."

I loved blaming Carol for things. She gave me an out, and why not use it? She owed me!

Eve said nothing again for a while, and then she said, "I just got the feeling you don't want a relationship with me." She looked sad, and I realized she had real feelings for me. I didn't want to hurt her.

"I'm just not emotionally available right now," I said plainly, "I don't have it to give, and I can understand if you don't think we should spend time together."

"I had a nice time," she said, catching me by surprise, "I just didn't get the sense you are that into me."

I wasn't. I didn't want to lie, but I didn't want to tell her the truth either.

"I like you," I said because it was true. I had no reason not to like her, "We just need to be friends and get to know each other, and I think it's important for your business relationship with my mom that we keep it that way. We don't need to rock the boat for your mom and mine. They have enough to deal with."

It was all true, and Eve agreed.

"You know," she commented reflectively, "I didn't expect you to be this nice to me. I thought it would be awkward between us from here on out, and I'm really glad it's not."

She took it well. I was relieved.

"Thanks for understanding," I said, and we called it an evening.

When I got home, Mom wanted to grill me about Eve, but I headed for my room and told her we'd talk later. I overheard her talking to Dad, and I wondered if they got along well living in the same house after all these years. Mom had her own room, but I found myself thinking about how awkward it must be for them.

I called Leo and made sure we were getting a significant delivery of Prime Meats at the restaurant, and I checked the numbers and realized things were on track for the grand opening after the damages were repaired and the steakhouse could reopen. I called Anna under the guise of business.

"We got lucky," she said, "We can reopen in a week. This coming Friday is perfect."

"I'll be there for it," I stated emphatically.

"You're flying up just for that?" She questioned my intentions.

"It's an important night. We need to do this right. I talked to Leo, and he's supplying us with a wide array of prime cuts of beef."

"Yippee," Anna said unenthusiastically.

"Look, you and I both know veganism is the way of the future, but it's premature. We can't get a thirty percent increase in sales with imitation hamburger, not just yet. We need to be smart about this and take it one step at a time," I explained.

"Spoken like a true businessman," she asserted.

"I have to ask you. Are you available on Friday to spend some time together?" I had to ask. I was compelled to ask. I had no choice but to ask. I had to know.

"What did you have in mind?" she asked glibly.

She had this way of making me sit on the edge of my chair in trepidation no matter what I said or did. I never knew what to think of it. Anna kept me perpetually on needles and pins.

"I want you to spend Friday night with me. I don't want you to leave. I want you to stay all night."

"I don't know," she hesitated a bit, "Raj might miss me too much."

That was hitting below the belt, and she had to know it.

"You told me you did whatever you like," I reminded her.

"What makes you think I would like to spend all Friday night with you?" she asked.

"Oh, something about what you and I have in common."

She laughed raucously, "Oh, you want to explore that further, do you?"

"I can't think of anything I'd rather do," I replied without hesitation.

"Do you think you might have an addiction problem?" she probed.

I knew she meant a sexual addiction, and it was strange to me since I had gone over a year without any sex at all.

"Maybe I'm just addicted to you," I suggested.

"That I can believe," she said, "Ok, Friday night it is. I'm all yours."

I was over the moon.

ᚦThirteen

It surprised me when I checked my messages, and there was one from Eve.

"I've been thinking about our conversation," she said, "And I'd like to explore a relationship with you even if it makes our moms uncomfortable. Let me know what you think. We can do this without putting the vegan cooking business at risk."

I had to think about that. Eve was understanding, empathetic, beautiful, and she wanted to have a relationship with me. She was from my home town and had similar values, yet she was different, and we had a lot in common, not least of which was our moms' shared business interests. Logic and reason suggested it was a good match. She was giving me a chance to make up my missteps with her, showing her compassion and forgiving side.

Anna, on the other hand, was engaged to another man, an animal rights activist running a steakhouse, which was a contradiction in terms, and she had no interest in having a relationship with me. The choice should have been easy, but that would be if logic and reason prevailed. They didn't. Lust and passion did.

I didn't respond to Eve. After all, I had plans with Anna, and I wanted to focus on the prime meats business. As much as Anna should have been opposed to my getting Leo more involved, she wasn't, and that added to her allure. If anything, she was helping me. I arranged a meeting in person with Leo and Anna at the restaurant when I arrived back in NYC for the weekend and the grand opening.

Things couldn't have gone off more splendidly. We were all dressed to the teeth for the event. I had never seen Anna sparkle so brightly. She wore form fitting yet elegant evening attire all day, even stiletto heels with little red bows on them. My eyes couldn't stop tracking her.

Leo showed up to check with the kitchen staff: the chef, sous-chef, and all the workers to discuss the meats, how to prepare them, and really sync up on the menu options. Anna was there and ultra attentive the whole time. I guess you could say she was on her "best behavior." She was professional with Leo to the extreme, asking questions, appearing to be impressed by the quality of the cuts of meat, and genuinely interested in every step of coordinating the new menus with the advertising to pull off the opening.

We had hired new staff, and Anna and Geneviève were both engaged in getting them up to speed. We decorated the place like New Years Eve with balloons and glitter and a big "grand reopening" sign out front. We also had online advertising happening, and we expected a large showing.

Early on, about 4:45 pm, the guests started arriving, and it went far beyond our expectations. The restaurant was rolling in every possible type of client from couples in romance-mode, to business execs entertaining colleagues, to families who loved steak; we were the "in" locale.

Anna was the most active I had ever seen her. She was at the front door with the new hostess making sure everything went according to plan. All the wait staff were properly attired in clean, pressed uniforms; all the new menus were nicely stacked in the right locations for wait staff to access them, the kitchen staff was on high alert to make the delicious prime meats steaks, and we had a large supply. All lights were green, and we were off!

I was actually enjoying myself, and Carl arrived a little after 6 pm.

"My flight was late," he announced, running in behind some guests.

"It's our night to shine!" I greeted him in my black suit with a bow tie.

"Jesus Christ! What a transformation! You have gotten with the program, my man!" Carl patted me on the back with two big thumps.

"I told you we could do this," I replied.

"Never a doubt in my mind, bro. You just had to have the right mind set. We are getting that thirty percent!"

Carl busied himself with talking to any staff who weren't deeply entrenched in work, and then he fraternized lightly with guests in a jovial manner. He even approached Anna and congratulated her on the hard work, and then he headed back to kitchen to check in with the food preparation team.

"This couldn't be going better," I commended Anna at around 7:30 pm when the restaurant and bar were full with a waiting list and packed entrance to the hostess station.

"I'm proud of you," she said, smiling at me.

"Proud of me?" I asked her.

"You really stepped up and took on this challenge. I know how much you wanted to do the vegan thing, and then you realized the time just wasn't right for it."

I didn't expect that much support from her. I was elated. I had hoped for success, but this was exceeding my expectations in spades.

One of the business men at the bar came up to me and introduced himself.

"I'm Elliott, and I'm impressed," he said.

"I'm Dan, and I'm glad you and your colleagues chose us for your dining pleasure."

"You're making a difference in this city of lights, my friend. I hear you have a vegan agenda."

"I would like to incorporate vegan options at some point, but for now, we're promoting prime meats, and we have quite a lineup tonight."

"I'm sure you do," Elliott voiced his approval, handing me his business card, "I'm a little old school. We could do this electronically, but I have a proposition for you on the vegan side that we can discuss. When you have the time, give me a call!"

"I'll do that," I promised.

This night was looking more and more promising. It exceeded all expectations. As the hours passed, it became livelier and livelier, and the staff was getting tired, but the tips were over the top, and they just worked harder. I retreated to the back office at one point to recover, and Anna followed me in.

She shut the door behind her and approached me standing in front of my desk. She pushed up flush against me, face-to-face and pressed me slightly bending backwards over my desk as she said, "Have you ever done it in your office?"

She didn't have to ask me twice. With one arm, I cleaned the desktop off, sending the items flying onto the floor, and she leaned into me, as I fully extended my back on the desk.

"Is the door locked?" I asked.

"Who cares?" she said, extending her hand to my crotch and fingering my genitals through the cloth. I was brought to attention in a way I had never been before.

I pushed her away for a second, stood up and said, "I do," as I walked to the door and locked it.

When I turned around, she had obviously had second thoughts, and she said, "I was just joking. We need to get back to work", and she walked to the door, unlocked it, and excited. For her, it was all about control. She had me again.

I sat at the desk unable to work, but I knew she had promised to spend the night with me, and I had that to look forward to.

Closing time was 10 pm, and Carl came into my office.

"What a night, bro!" he exclaimed, "I'm staying with you at the apartment, dude, I didn't get a hotel."

I hadn't thought about that. Sure, there was a spare bedroom, but he'd see Anna unless I was careful about it, and I wasn't sure how I felt about that.

"Can I run the numbers from here and then join you later?" Carl asked, "I want to make sure we hit the mark on profitability; send me a few emails, and then I'll join you?"

I was still working out the logistics. Then suddenly, I knew what to do.

"Actually, you do that, and here's the key," I tossed it to him, "I have to go over to the police station and meet with the detective tonight."

"Are you serious? It's after 10 pm. They won't be open."

"We have an appointment, and it's a private meeting, but don't wait up for me. Just run the numbers, send the reports, and get some sleep. We'll sync up in the morning."

"Whatever you say," Carl confirmed, as he set up his tablet computer and got to work, "but why is all your stuff on the floor?" He pointed at the items from the desk that I had knocked off when Anna had suggested we "do it" on the desktop.

I just shook my head.

I had completed the first part; now I had to get to Anna.

She was in the dining room checking in with staff for the night and making sure everything was cleaned up.

I walked up to her and whispered in her ear, "Can we meet at your place instead of mine? Carl wants to stay there," I said, sure she would understand, but still a little considered and nervous.

"Oh ... you don't want to make it a threesome?"

I didn't know how to respond, even though the answer was clear to me. No way.

"Ha ha, very funny," I said, hoping it was meant as a joke, "I want you all to myself."

"In that case, sure," she said, "I'm ready when you are."

Things were really going my way!

Anna and I departed for her place. As we were walking, I had a sense we were being followed. There was a black limo driving near us, cars honking and driving around it, and it seemed to be keeping pace with us. Just as I was beginning to feel really uncomfortable, someone jumped out of it, ran towards me, threw a burlap bag over my head, knocked me off my feet and drug me into the limo.

Completely unawares and confused, I struggled to breathe, but I calmed myself. I needed to stay alert to figure out what was happening.

I began to wonder if they had Anna too and where we were going. I could hear people speaking in what I was sure was Russian, or maybe Polish or Hungarian; what did I know? It was harsh, crisp and clear, if only I spoke the language.

There was something around my neck restricting my movement, and my arms were tied behind my back. I relaxed my breath and realized I was not going to pass out or be asphyxiated, so I stayed vigilant and alert to what would happen next.

After a few minutes the car pulled over, and I was taken out and escorted, with the burlap bag still over my head, to some location that was indoors. As the door opened, I heard a voice with the same strong, presumably Russian accent say, "Lift your feet."

I followed the directions and entered the room. I could hear the beeping sounds of an elevator, and I was nudged forward to enter after a short wait. I could hear more beeping, and it seemed that we were going up a number of levels, and then the elevator stopped, and whoever was in the elevator with me escorted me out and into another doorway where the escorts disappeared, and the door behind me closed. I was surprised at how calm I felt, but then I realized there was nothing I could do, so there was no reason to feel any other way. It was just the calm before the storm.

Someone came near me and untied my arms and loosened the grip around my neck, and a woman's voice instructed me, "Please bend forward a bit," and I did. She lifted the bag over my head, and it fell off onto the floor. I looked up, and there was an older woman, maybe in her sixties, about 4'10", standing in front of me, speaking with a strong Russian accent.

"Please take a seat," she said as she walked around to her desk and took a seat herself. I looked around, hoping there was a way I could identify the place, but it was pristinely clean with neutral colors, no decorations, and nothing signature about it. There was an empty bookshelf, and a big window, but it was dark outside, and the blinds were drawn.

The woman seated behind the desk said, "My name is Natasha, and I won't take much of your time."

I thought that was the oddest thing to say, but since she said it, I did feel somewhat relieved. If she was being polite about my time, maybe I had some time left to my life.

"You are here because we saw you with Anna Hobart at the steakhouse, and we are concerned."

Another odd statement.

"Who's 'we'?" I asked innocently.

"That is not your concern, but this might be," Natasha said, displaying a photo on a small screen from a smart device.

I squinted to look closely at it from across the table. It was definitely a concern for me. It was a picture of Eve, my mom and her mom.

"What the HELL?" I shouted in outrage, almost leaping out of the chair.

"Calm down or we put the bag back on," Natasha stated matter-of-factly.

I began to wonder who else was outside the door because I could take this 4'10" Russian grandma down with one punch and escape.

"What do you want?" I asked in desperation.

"It's what you want," she said, "You don't want your female friends to be hurt, do you?"

She was obviously threatening me. I said nothing.

"The way to avoid that is to do what we ask."

"Which is?" I asked with my mouth agape.

"We want you to observe Anna and report back to us on her activities."

"Seriously?" I began to think this was some kind of a joke, "You want me to spy on Anna?"

"We will put a wire on you so you can record your conversations with her, and we can listen."

"Who are you? The KGB or something?" I asked, waving my arms around.

She laughed, "The KGB collapsed in 1991, but you've heard of that?"

"In crazy late-night movies!" I defended my lack of knowledge with more ignorance.

"Now it's the FSB," Natasha explained.

"And that would be you?" I asked naively.

"No, definitely not."

We were back at square one.

"Let me get this straight. You want me to wear a wire to spy on Anna Hobart and report back to you, but I don't even get to know who you are or why?"

"But you do buy protection for these women," she lifted the smart device screen photo of mom, Eve and Roberta again to eye level.

"This is ridiculous," I said, shaking my head.

"Look," Natasha went further, "We want to make this as simple as possible. If you do what we ask, you don't have to worry. Nothing bad will happen to you or your friends and family," she clarified.

"Unless I consider Anna to be a friend?" I asked, surprising myself at just how much I was keeping my wits about me.

"Do you consider Anna a friend?" Natasha asked.

This was getting too deep and personal for me.

"I'd like to keep her a friend and not an enemy, that's for sure. I don't think spying on her is a great way to do that," I said.

Natasha heaved a loud sigh. "All right," she said, getting up and making her way to the door; she opened it and let in an over seven foot tall man with a mustache and ample body hair except for on his bald head. He looked at me with a somber stare, and I couldn't help but notice his bulging muscles and strong arms and legs. He could destroy me with one blow.

"All right," I said, "I'll do it."

"That's better," Natasha said, "Igor, you can go," and she escorted the power body builder / henchman out the door.

"It's much better this way," she said.

"None of this is good," I said knowingly and prepared for the instructions on what I had to do to spy on Anna and protect my loved ones.

☙ FOURTEEN

I was dropped off down the street from my apartment, and I was hoping Carl had arrived and let Anna in, but I really didn't know what to expect. I had my marching orders from Natasha that I had grudgingly accepted, but I was hoping to spend a little quality time with Anna and tell her what I had been instructed to. Instead, when I knocked on the door (noticed that it was 2 am), no one answered. Luckily, I had hid a second key on a small string inside my mailbox that had a number pad to get in for emergencies.

It was completely quiet when I entered, and I wondered if Carl and Anna were even there. Maybe Anna had gone back to her place? Maybe Carl was sleeping? I cautiously walked to the main room with the waterbed and noted the door was closed. That was strange because I had left it open when I left.

Carl had visited before and knew where the spare bedroom was, this being the main one, so I just turned the knob and opened the door. To my horror, Anna and Carl were lying in the bed locked in each other's arms, facing each other asleep.

"What the FUCK!" I screamed at the top of my lungs and Carl jolted awake and sat up in bed.

Anna moved her arm as he jolted up and turned over, continuing to sleep.

"God, bro, you scared me!" Carl shouted in earnest.

"I scared you? You're fucking Anna in my bed!" I accused him angrily.

"What difference does it make to you?" Carl asked, obviously not knowing anything about my situation with Anna, and that was my choice. She had notably not said anything to him about our previous encounters either, and she wasn't even disturbed enough at my entrance to sit up in bed. How could she just keep sleeping through this?

"We'll talk in the morning," I said, closing the door and making my way to the spare bedroom. What difference did it make? I was now officially spying on Anna. How could I possibly have a real relationship with her even if she wanted one?

I lay in bed in the spare room with my mind doing summersaults. I had all kinds of questions. Who was Anna and why were these Russians following her anyway? Natasha had explained to me that when I was kidnapped Anna had also had a burlap bag placed on her head, and she had been taken to a different location and told that I was involved in some nefarious activities and that she had to spy on me. Natasha said they did this so that she wouldn't know they were on to her. She was also told that if she didn't wear a wire and spy on me, she would have consequences like harm coming to her fiancé, Raj. For some odd reason I took pleasure in this conundrum. What would tomorrow bring? In a fit of internal turbulence, I eventually fell into a restless slumber.

In the morning, I heard someone in the kitchen, and I leaped up. I ran out of my room, but when I got to the kitchen, I was disappointed to find only Carl.

"Where is she?"

"Anna? She left like in the wee hours. Here's a note."

True to her typical style, Anna had left early without confronting us. The note said, "Had a great time with you boys. See you!"

"I just don't get it," I said to Carl, "What gives with her 'devil-may-care' audacity to just play with us like this?"

"What are you talking about?" Carl asked, rummaging around in the refrigerator hoping to find milk that wasn't sour, "Do you even care if there's fresh milk? Are you using oat milk or soy milk or something like that now?" he asked, as if it mattered.

"Look, bro, we shouldn't be sleeping with Anna," I scolded.

"We?" he asked.

"You saw me flirting with her. You knew we had it going on," I accused playfully, making myself some toast. No need for milk of any kind.

"You denied it, dude. If you had your eye on her, and she was off limits to me, you should have said something. You didn't."

That was true.

"So, how was it?" I asked.

"Oh, kiss and tell?" Carl asked, "Sorry, not doing that."

"I mean, did you just jump into bed with her?" I was genuinely curious how their situation compared to mine with Anna. After all, I did have to spy on her.

"I didn't see it coming, actually. I got back here late, like 11:30 pm. I let myself in with the key you left me, and I was in bed sleeping."

"In the main bedroom?" I asked inquisitively.

"I forgot about the spare bedroom. I was tired, and I just jumped in the first bed. Anna must have come in later, like after midnight when I was asleep, and she jumped into bed with me. I didn't see it coming. I woke up hugging her. It was super awkward. She said something like 'you told me you wanted me to stay all night with you. Here I am.' Weird, huh?"

I appreciated the play-by-play. So, Anna thought she was climbing in bed with me!

"So, what happened in the morning?" I asked.

"I didn't hear her leave. I just got up and found this note on the table and started making breakfast. Then you arrived."

It made sense on some level now. At least Carl wasn't having sex with Anna. At least not yet, but I had to be sure.

"So, you didn't have sex with her?"

"Not that I'm aware of ..." he let his sentence suggest otherwise. Typical Carl.

Then he said, "You gotta check the financials, dude. I sent them to you and Don. They are spectacular!"

I smiled. At least one thing was on target.

After breakfast, Carl took a cab to the airport, and I stayed back to try to make sense of this. I wanted to find out what was going on in Anna's head.

I made my way to the restaurant, and after the grand re-opening, there was plenty of work to do. Anna was there meeting with the chef and sous-chef when I arrived.

"Good morning, all!" I shouted.

Anna came over to me, "Let's talk in your office."

I followed her in, and this time she cared about locking the door.

"Last night I was kidnapped," she confided.

"You don't say," I said calmly.

"Someone threw a burlap bag over my head and took me to some weird office somewhere in the city, and then this guy asked me to spy on you."

I was taken aback by her honesty. I hadn't been planning to come clean on my end.

"He said if I didn't do it, they'd do something to Raj."

"If you didn't do what?" I asked, mostly because I wanted to sync up her story with Natasha's version.

"Agree to follow you and report back to them."

"Who's them?" This I also wanted her take on.

"Someone who has an interest in some suspicious activities you are involved in."

"Suspicious activities that I'm involved in?" I repeated her words.

"Well, I'm not going to do it!" she yelled, losing her normal tried and true calm.

I couldn't ask if she was wearing a wire because I was, and I didn't want her to ask.

"Look, I'm not involved in anything illegal."

"Tell them that!" she yelled at me a second time.

"Who's 'them'?" I asked again.

"I have no idea, but someone motivated enough to kidnap me. What happened to you?"

Natasha had informed me that we were grabbed at exactly the same moment, so Anna didn't know I had had the same burlap bag treatment, freeing me to tell her something different.

"Do you remember when you and I were walking to my apartment, and a limo was following us?"

"Yes, I do remember that," she said, following my train of thought closely.

"Well, the limo swerved and came towards us on the sidewalk, and I was almost hit by it, but you were on the inside, so I jumped to get out of the way, and it continued past you, but I guess at that point you had been grabbed by the kidnapper during the limo drive by incident, which must have been intentional to get access to you because you disappeared. I looked back after the limo drove away, and you were gone without a trace," I explained in a way that I hoped sounded plausible.

"I was unable to see so I really don't know what kind of vehicle I was in, but somehow, I was taken away and then after I was forced to agree to spy on you, I was dropped off back at your place. That's when I was going to knock on the door, but you had left it open. I was surprised, so I went in and locked it and went to the bedroom, assuming that was you in the master bedroom sleeping, so I climbed in bed, but it was Carl! He turned towards me, and I was telling him I was back to spend the night, thinking it was you. When I saw it was Carl, I just turned over and went to sleep. I was exhausted, and I just figured I'd tell you about it in the morning."

I realized she was being honest, which made me feel very self-conscious about wearing a wire. She didn't ask me more about it. I felt compelled to tell her the truth, so I took a piece of paper and wrote, "I'm wearing a wire." I showed it to her. She opened her eyes widely, and I opened my shirt and pointed at it. I didn't want to take it off and risk alerting them, especially since they had threatened the women in my life.

"So, are we good?" she asked, and I knew she was referencing the wire and making sure I wasn't in trouble.

"Yes," I answered emphatically, "Can we have a makeover tonight?" I asked.

"Absolutely," she said, enthusiastically this time. The drama seemed to intrigue her.

I got through the rest of the day one way or another. I met up with Anna for dinner at the steakhouse. We both ordered entrées and sat at a table in the back.

"I have good news – revenues are skyrocketing! We were up forty percent for the re-opening, and I'm hoping to keep that trend moving. With the five-star reviews we're getting, word of mouth and online re-ferral, we shouldn't have any problem sustaining that trend!"

"That's good to hear," she said, being noticeably careful due to the wire.

I reached under my shirt and undid the wire, took it off, showed it to her, disconnected, and put it away.

"I think we need a break from this," I said, putting it in my back pocket. She smiled.

"So, you did that for me?" she asked.

"What's that?" I wanted to know which part she appreciated.

"You removed the wire for me and told me about it. You could've kept it a secret and just protected your loved ones."

"I certainly hope they're in no danger. The gal that talked to me during the kidnapping was even threatening my mom!" I didn't men-tion Eve and Roberta.

"Well, we're safe now," Anna said, smiling and leaning in towards me as she finished her veggie melt, one of the new items on the menu. I was having a New York steak. She didn't seem to care or notice, and then she took her foot and began to rub it against my ankle under the table. I could get used to staring into those pale, mesmerizing, intoxi-cating blue eyes of hers. I was going crazy.

This time we took a cab to my place. I was taking no chances on more kidnappings. When we arrived, I made sure to lock the front door. We were home free. I went to use the restroom, and when I came out, Anna was ready for me. She was sprawled on top of the waterbed com-forter in a purple satin bralette and thong. She had nylons with lacy tops mid-way up her thighs and black stilettos and a garter belt on. I didn't think she could get sexier, but she had. I was imagining what it would be like with her, as I had been for months now, and finally we were together, and it was happening. My dreams had come true! Getting kidnapped seemed like a small price to pay.

I walked out, fully clothed, and approached the bed, and then I just stopped and took it all in: her hair softly gliding down past her shoulders, her perfect smile, her gorgeous, slim body, lying spread out on my bed in rapture. She was beautiful, intriguing, exciting, and classy. I didn't care if we didn't have a relationship. I didn't mind if I had to get my head covered in a burlap bag. I didn't mind having my family threatened. I could handle it as long as I had Anna to come home to.

There was a knock at the door. I thought about ignoring it, but it got louder. The tapping turned to pounding. What could it be? I had to answer it. I told Anna to be quiet and stay in the bedroom, and I closed the bedroom door as I made my way to the main door. My intention was to get rid of whoever it was quickly and get back to business.

When I opened the door, I came face to face with Igor.

"Hi there, Dan," he said.

I felt like slamming the door in his face, but I controlled myself.

"Why aren't you wearing the wire?" he asked. He didn't skip a beat.

"Come on..." I chided.

"I thought we had a deal. Didn't we have a deal? You wouldn't want anyone to get hurt?"

How was I going to get out of this one? I wasn't. But would Anna have sex with me if I was wearing a wire?

"I hesitate to wear it during certain activities," I said, alluding to something private but not wanting to come right out and say it.

"Those are the ones we want to capture most," Igor elaborated, "That's when people sometimes say things they wouldn't say otherwise."

Great, Igor was going to listen to Anna come and confess something about her activities that he and Natasha would find interesting. What had I gotten myself into?

"All right, I'll put it on right away," I agreed.

He smiled, "I knew you wouldn't want me to have to come back and explain it again."

I locked the door, got the wire out of my pocket, and opened the bedroom door. Anna was on her hands and knees like a cat with her bum in the air.

I took the device around to her face and showed it to her.

"That was one of the henchmen. I have to wear this."

"Ok," she said, "Let's give them a good show."

I laughed and took off all my clothes, including my underwear, and I attached the device up high by my chest and turned it on.

"Take me from behind," Anna invited, "Fuck me like a bitch."

By bitch, I assumed she meant a she-dog, and her behavior made me feel like a raging bull. I put on a rubber and got behind her on my knees on the bed.

"Grab my ass, and hump me from behind," she instructed.

I felt her firm, tight buttocks, and I found myself immediately aroused.

I took the fingers of my right hand and felt her sex. She was tight and lightly wet as if perspiring. It was a huge turn on.

I got up on my haunches and penetrated her from behind, pulling her cheeks apart as she lifted herself towards me. I entered her sweet spot and breathed a wide, expansive breath of air,giving me chills down my spine.

"Ahhhh," Anna emitted a long sigh of pleasure, like the purr of a cat, and it turned me on savagely.

"I want you to come," I said, fingering her clitoris while riding her from behind.

"Make me come," she whispered.

I rubbed her clit with tiny circular motions in both directions, and then up and down slowly at first and then more vigorously as I stroked her from behind methodically, slowly, giving her my full length, and then faster and furiously as I felt myself getting so turned on, I couldn't control it. I scaled it back to continue longer, and she was shaking and moving fluidly with my touch.

"Rub my tits," she instructed.

I took my right hand off her clit, steadying myself with my left hand as I rubbed her stiff nipple and cupped her breast and fondled it. She pulled her head back and sighed, purring like a cat. She arched her back, and I switched hands, using my right hand to steady myself and my left hand to rub her left nipple and fondle her left breast, and then I drug my hand gently over her sternum and up her throat and stroked her front like a feline. She made cooing noises like a bird.

I couldn't control myself any longer. I sprung off of her and flipped her over aggressively. I was on top, and I fingered her crotch through her panties. She was getting wetter and wiggling with delight. I had never seen Anna so excited. I wondered if it was me or the idea that I was wearing a wire and people were listening in to us that was making her so hot.

She lifted her legs still in stilettos and spread them widely, as I positioned myself on top of her and drove myself fully into her, becoming one with her. When I was deeply inside of her, I came down in front, spreading my legs out behind me and drawing my chest flush to her chest, tickling her breasts with my touch, as I looked deeply into her eyes. I was in love.

We moved together, Anna arching her back and making small circles with my body as connected to her as was humanly possible. She started to buck against me and then move in circles again, going in the opposite direction, and then she moved against me yet again, whimpering like a kitten. She was getting warmer and wetter, and then she began bucking me like a wild bronco, and she drove her fingernails into my back, sharp and firm, tearing the flesh.

She screamed out, "Dan, you're fucking making me come!"

Her whole body jerked and riveted alternatively, taking me with her like a ride on the ocean. I let go and went with her on the journey, borderless and boundaryless, releasing all tension, all concerns of this world, and any reservations I had. I was meant for this moment, and

Anna was all mine. I screamed out, and when I came, it was an out of body experience.

We lay next to each other in bliss. Holding hands, faces up in silence. I wondered what Igor and Natasha thought of us now, not that it mattered to me.

"I love you, Anna," I said because I meant it.

She purred, and we went to sleep.

FIFTEEN

My mom left several messages for me. I decided to return them the next day.

"Hi, Mom."

"Worried about you, Dan. When are you coming home?"

"I'm in the apartment here in NYC, Mom. Things are going well, and I decided to stay for a few days."

"I get that, but I'd like your help with the new vegan cooking school business. Roberta and I are doing well, but Eve has been asking about you."

"Yeah, Mom, about that ..."

"Look," Mom interrupted me, "I know your personal life isn't my business."

"You got that right," I chimed in to give her a hint.

"But you have to think about this, Dan," she counseled me.

"I know, Mom, I'm not getting any younger. You want grandkids."

"Not just that," Mom said, "I really think Eve could be good for you. She's beautiful; she kind; she really likes you."

"I understand, Mom, I'll be honest. I'm not that into her."

Silence.

"Mom?"

"Then why did you have sex with her?" Mom asked.

Ok, now we were crossing lines.

"Look, Mom, you just said you understood that my personal life is none of your business."

"Don't be like your father," Mom persisted, and I had a feeling I didn't want to hear this, "Sex and love are one and the same. You can't use someone for sex."

I found myself hoping Anna was taking note and wondering what Igor and Natasha thought of my conversation with my mom since I was still wearing the wire.

"Mom, I didn't know at the time that I wasn't into Eve. She's nice. I just don't feel that

connected to her."

"Give her a chance," Mom begged, "Why don't you come to Tampa for a while?"

I thought about it. I was enjoying my time with Anna; I was near the Prime Meats businesses I needed to build, and I was loving the excitement, but Mom was right. I had agreed to help her and Roberta with the business, and I did owe Eve a response to her earlier phone message.

"All right," I agreed, "I'll come home and help."

"You'll be glad you did!" Mom spouted encouragement.

Anna had me over for dinner at her place before I flew out. She had candles on the tables and made vegan food, but it wouldn't have mattered if she fed me manure, and we sat in her bathtub. I was in love.

We stared into each other's eyes, and Cruella came up and nibbled at my toes and licked my feet with her harsh, rough tongue. I was part of the family.

After dinner, Anna and I did get into her bathtub. It was a stand-alone one with the little legs on the tile, and both of us fit. We each sat on one end, staring at each other. I couldn't continue to wear the wire in the water, so I strategically placed it outside the tub.

"Why did you become an animal rights activist?" I asked her.

"It's something I feel strongly about," she said, perhaps feeling more open and vulnerable because we were both naked in the tub together and had just made love for the third time in two days.

"Did you always feel that way?" I asked.

"No, as a child I didn't think about it, but one day I realized just how ridiculous it is that we kill animals for no reason when we could easily get our nutrition from plants."

"So why work at a steakhouse?"

"I don't know. I was looking for a job, and managing restaurants comes easily to me. In a city like New York, you're going to make more money at a steakhouse than you would at a health food venue. Like you said, nobody pays big bucks for a tofu sandwich."

I laughed.

"What about you? Why are you following an animal rights activist around while you run a prime meats agenda?"

"You, I find fascinating," I responded, "I've never met someone I so profoundly connect to on every level. You make me question what I do, what I stand for, who I am. You make me whole."

She laughed. "That's profound in and of itself."

"It's true," I said, realizing I was leaving myself exposed.

"What did I do to deserve you?" Anna asked.

I had never thought of it that way. I always thought she just got off on controlling me. I didn't realize there was another side to it.

"I don't know, but you have me," I said, "Except I have to fly back to Tampa tonight to help my mom run a vegan food kitchen."

"That sounds enticing," she remarked.

I didn't want to go, but I reluctantly parted ways with Anna and flew home to Tampa. It was depressing, but I knew I had to do it. I met up with Mom, Robert and Eve in the dark kitchen.

Mom hugged me, "How was your flight?"

"Tiring," I confided, "but ok. Glad to be home."

Roberta came up and hugged me, and then Eve came up and did the same.

"Did you get my message?" she asked.

"I did," I replied, noticing she was looking down, "It was nice. We'll talk later."

She smiled.

I helped out by tasting some of the entrées and weighing in with my two cents; we tweaked some of the recipes and discussed go to market strategies.

"How are the classes coming along?" I asked Roberta.

"So far, so good. Enrollment is up. We go live this week, and then we'll complete the first class and do some student surveys, but I have a suspicion it will go well."

I smiled.

"The cruise lines in particular are important. If they do well, we'll get to train their whole teams in several cities, New York, San Francisco, and Tampa."

"That's great!" I chimed in. I got the feeling they didn't need much from me and that the invitation to come home was more about talking to Eve.

After the meeting, Eve asked me to walk her to her car.

"Dan, what do you think of my proposal?" she asked.

"I like you, Eve, but I really haven't changed my mind," I said as we neared her car, "I want to help you and Roberta and my mom with the business, but I'm actually dating someone else."

Her face fell, and I felt really bad about it, but at least I was being honest now.

"What is it about me?" she asked.

"I like you," I admitted, "I just think romantically I'm interested in someone else."

"So why did you have sex with me then?" she asked.

This was a tough one. I wished I had a better answer.

"Honestly, Eve, we're young. We're going to sleep with different people, but we have to find the one person that makes living worthwhile."

"And I just don't do that for you?"

"I don't know, but I have a relationship with someone else," I said, attempting to be as truthful as I could.

"Did you have that relationship when we went out?"

I wasn't sure why it mattered, but at this point, I had to respond. We were standing outside by her car, and I was deciding what to say when a car pulled up beside me and a man rolled down his window and said, "How's it going Dan?"

It was Igor. What was he doing in Tampa? I was still wearing the wire.

"I'm fine; how are you?" I asked, not flinching and attempting to keep my composure.

He smiled and drove away.

"Who was that?" Eve asked.

I tried not to show any side of foul play.

"Nobody, Eve," I smiled, "I have to go now."

When I got home, Dad and Mom were together in the kitchen talking.

"Hey, son, how's the gig in New York?" Dad asked.

I took a seat beside them at the table.

"Great, dad, I'm enjoying it."

"How are things with you and Eve?" Mom asked.

Dad looked intrigued, "A new girlfriend?"

It was my chance to set things right.

"Dad, remember how Carl told her there was a woman in NYC that I had a "thing" for, and I denied it?"

Dad nodded, "Yes, I remember that."

"Well, I do have a thing for her, and she's staying in the apartment with me."

Mom didn't know this, and she had a sour look on her face, "You didn't mention this!" she challenged.

"Remember that talk we had about you minding your own business?" I asked, "I'll introduce her to you when the time is right."

Dad smiled, "Like father, like son."

Mom kicked him under the table.

"What does that mean?" I asked.

"Your mother and I had a 'thing' going on for a while, and my family thought I was dating a different girl, but for me, it was always your mom. I knew right away even though she wasn't interested in me."

Mom said nothing.

"See," I chided, "when the shoe's on the other foot, how do you like it exposing your personal life to me?"

"It's not the same thing," she said, shaking her head.

We all laughed, and I went to my room. I realized I would always be their son, and they would be concerned about me. I just had to learn to live with that.

The phone rang, and I answered it.

"What happened to Anna?" the voice said.

"Who is this?" I replied forcefully.

"Where is she?" the voice persisted.

"In New York City," I answered, figuring it was evasive enough that it wouldn't matter who was asking.

"Do we have to prove to you that we mean business?" the voice asked.

It wasn't Natasha's or Igor's voice. Who was it?

"I didn't do anything. To my knowledge Anna is where she's supposed to be."

"You better find her and FAST," the voice prompted.

I didn't know why, but I had a funny feeling I had to do something about it.

I called Anna, and the phone went to voicemail.

"Call me as soon as you get this," I said to the recording, "We need to talk."

Sixteen

Carl and I were at the sports bar enjoying nachos and beers. It was just like the good old days.

"I'm sorry I accused you of going after Anna," I started, "I am seeing her."

"Really?" he seemed surprised, "I thought you weren't that into her."

"I didn't want you to know, but yeah, we're seeing each other. Hands off!"

"OK, but what about Eve?" Carl asked.

"Come on!" I shouted, "Is my mom talking to you about her?"

"Hey, I've lived in this town and known your family too long for you to pull a fast one on me, Dan. Of course I know what's going on! Everyone knows that Roberta's daughter has a thing for you and has for years, and she's pretty cute."

"She may be cute, but I'm into Anna. Why don't you date her?"

"Not my type, bro," Carl answered without a second thought.

"Ok, what's your type?" I prodded.

"She's pretty, but she's timid and unsure of herself. I like a take charge woman," he explained.

"Ok, so now I see why you're jealous of me and Anna."

"Not jealous, bro, you asked my 'type', and I told you."

"Ok, that's fair," I said.

My phone rang. I hadn't told Carl about Igor and Natasha, and I didn't want to.

I answered it, plugging one ear because the sports bar was noisy.

"We warned you," the voice said, "No Anna, we go after the girls."

"What girls?" I asked, fully understanding the voice was referring to my mom, Roberta and Eve. When Igor had driven by the night before when we were at her car, I should have been more concerned. I had wondered why some Russian thug had time to go from NYC to Tampa to chase a young guy with an MBA and threaten him? There had to be more to this story. Just what was at stake here? What didn't I know about Anna? Was my lust coloring my judgment?

He hung up.

"Carl, I have to go," I said, heading for the exit.

"Dude, you are just one mysterious moment after another," he said.

"I'll call you!" I said, making a run to my car. I headed for the dark kitchen.

Mom, Roberta and Eve were all there. I was pleased to see that. The class was in session, but there was a strange man in the class, a Latino dude with slicked black hair, overly well dressed for Tampa, and he didn't appear to know much about cooking.

"Who's that?" I asked Roberta, pointing at the guy, "He doesn't look like a chef."

"He's one of the students from the cruise line," Roberta explained, "He doesn't have to be a chef. They send us anyone who wants to learn how to cook vegan, and some of them are here just to see how we teach."

"That's great," I said, not wanting to scare Roberta.

I looked over at Eve who was talking to the guy. They looked a little too chummy. Then Eve turned to Roberta and said, "Patricio and I are going to get something to eat."

That seemed strange. They were eating here.

"Why don't you stay and have some the vegan food with the other students?" I asked.

Eve walked up to me and whispered in my ear, "Patricio wants to take me on a date. He's interested in me even if you're not."

She walked away from me, towards Patricio. Alarm bells went off, but I didn't have the right words to say. I couldn't tell her some thug had threatened to hurt her, my mom and her mom because I wasn't keeping close enough tabs on my girlfriend who I preferred to her. It wouldn't make sense, and I knew better than to try. She'd just think I was somehow desperately trying to have sex with both of them.

Instead, I turned to Roberta, "Do you think it's a good idea for Eve to date Patricio?" I asked.

She laughed, "My daughter never listens to me when it comes to men."

Eve and Patricio walked out. I followed them. "Where are you two going?" I asked. Eve looked at me quizzically.

Patricio answered, "Grab a bite at that Mexican place up the street."

"I love that place," I said, "Mind if I tag along?"

Patricio looked a bit distraught, and his whole demeanor changed, "Look, I want to get know the lovely lady a little better, dude, you're cramping my style."

Unfortunately, Eve didn't know enough to take my side.

"He's right, Dan," she said, "You had your chance. I'd like to have dinner with Patricio alone."

"All right," I said, "Call me if you need me. You have my number."

She gave me a strange look, "That's not going to happen."

I called my mom and she answered. "Don't leave yet, Mom. I'm coming to get you."

I headed back to the dark kitchen, checking my phone, no messages from Anna. I called the steakhouse. Geneviève answered. "May I speak to Anna please?"

"She's not here," Geneviève said, "She was scheduled for tonight, and it's not like her not only not to show up, but she didn't even call to check on us."

I hung up and called Carl. "I need to ask you a favor, buddy."

"What's that?"

"You know that Mexican restaurant down the street on Hugo?" I asked.

"Yeah ... the one by that new dark kitchen space where your mom works?"

"Yep, I need you to go there and keep an eye on Eve and a Latino guy going by the name of Patricio."

"Come on, dude, now you're following Eve? I didn't think you had a thing for her."

"It's not that, Carl, I need your help. Someone is going to hurt her."

"Ok, ok, relax, dude. I'm on it. I'll call you and let you know what I find," Carl replied.

I headed over to pick up Mom at the kitchen. When I got there, the place was quiet. I looked around, and all the students were gone, which made it sense, the class had ended, but Roberta and Mom usually hung around to tidy up before leaving. It was unlike them to take off so quickly, and besides, I had called Mom and asked her to wait.

I picked up my phone to call her when someone tapped me on the back. I turned around. It was Igor.

"Come with me, Danny Boy," he said, "Some people just have to learn the hard way."

"I don't know what you are talking about!" I shouted at him.

Igor grabbed me by the ear and pulled, "Then I'll show you firsthand."

And he drug me out of the building.

SEVENTEEN

Once outside, Igor let go of my ear, but he whispered it, "Do as I say, or someone might get hurt."

I paused. There was no instruction. I looked up at him. "Yes?"

He didn't seem very good at intimidating people. He used his size, and he did look threatening, but he didn't have his tactics down, and I wondered why that was.

"Just keep walking," he instructed, and I did. He led me to a van with darkened windows, and he put me in the back. "No funny business!" he said. He handcuffed and blindfolded me. I could talk to him, so I didn't feel completely helpless, but I couldn't see where he was taking me.

He drove for a few minutes; then, he opened the door and led me out, but he didn't remove the blindfold until I heard a door open, and my mother say, "Oh, thank God!"

"What is happening?" I shouted. At that moment, Igor untied my hands and took off my blindfold. Mom, Roberta, and Eve were all in chairs with their feet and hands restrained, seated a few feet apart.

"I don't get it!" I shouted desperately, "What is going on? Why are you doing this?"

Roberta was looking straight ahead, expressionless. My mother looked like she had been crying. Eve was trembling and looked terrified.

I was standing at the doorway with a wide stance looking at everyone, and I couldn't believe my eyes. It made no sense to me.

Natasha was standing in the back of the room, and she said, "Where is Anna?"

"How the hell would I know?" I asked, "What makes you people think I have some kind of control over her?"

Igor said, "You agreed to wear a wire and track her, and we told you that your mother, her friend, and her daughter were in danger if you didn't do what you said you would do."

My mother looked at my puzzled, "Is that true?"

Eve looked up at me and asked, "Who's Anna?"

Roberta continued to look straight ahead and said nothing.

"This isn't getting us anywhere," I pleaded with Igor and Natasha. I noticed Patricio was also standing in the back of the room with Natasha, "I left a message for Anna, and she didn't return the call. I don't know what you want me to do."

"Did you tip her off?" Patricio asked.

"To what? That she was being followed?"

"Yes," Natasha perpetuated Patricio's line of questioning, "Did you tell her you were wearing a wire?"

I knew my answer was not a good one. I hesitated, and I saw a vision of someone torturing me saying, "We have ways of making you talk!" in a German accent. I just had no idea who it was, and I was hoping it wasn't a foreshadowing.

"Tell me who Anna is!" Eve howled.

"She's a woman who manages a restaurant in NYC," I answered.

"Are you fucking her?" Eve asked.

Now was definitely not the time for the jealous would-be girlfriend to get emotional.

"What difference does it make to you? You wanted to date what's-his-name," I motioned with my head in Patricio's direction.

My phone rang. It was Carl.

Everyone looked at me.

"Answer it!" Natasha said, "Maybe it's Anna."

"It's Carl," I said, and I picked it up, "Now's not a good time, dude."

"What are you talking about?" Carl replied, "You told me to follow Eve and that Hispanic guy for you, but I can't find them anywhere."

"It doesn't matter anymore," I said matter-of-factly because it didn't.

"Dude, you are so out of line. First, you call me and ask me for a favor, and then you pull this."

"Believe me, Carl. I have bigger problems now. Just be glad you're not here with me."

"I don't know how to respond to that," Carl said, "but you'll never believe who just walked through the door."

"Now's not the time, Carl," I pleaded with him to let it go.

"Anna, dude, she's here in Tampa," and of course, Igor, Natasha, Patricio and all the ladies could hear.

"Tell him to follow her," Igor said.

"Who's that?" Carl asked.

"Look, Carl, you're at the Mexican restaurant, right?"

"Of course, bro, it's where you told me to go! Jesus!"

Sometimes you realize your life has become a comedy. "Stay there. Try to engage Anna in conversation."

"Wait! Dude!"

I hung up.

"Igor, she's here. We just have to get her."

"You go get her," Igor said, "All your lady friends, Natasha, Frank and I will be here waiting for you."

Apparently, Patricio's real name was Frank.

I took one last look at everyone, taking stock of all the emotion in the room, and I said, "I'll get her and bring her back."

"Make it quick!" Igor said, "You know what's at stake."

It left me wondering what Igor could possibly be considering doing to my mother, Roberta, and Eve, but I didn't dare to go there. I didn't have the gift of time on my side.

I took off running. I noticed where we were, but then I had been blindfolded, so when I got to the street, I realized it was a ten minute or longer walk to the restaurant where Carl saw Anna. I booked a Lift on my smartphone and waited. It only took five minutes, but it felt like five minutes too long.

"Take me to Pedro's," I said to the driver, "You'll get a bigger tip if you get me there faster."

I took note of the location we were leaving from. It was a building on the outskirts of town that I wasn't familiar with, but I certainly knew how to get back. I did recognize the neighborhood. I could have sworn Dad had a client in this neck of the woods. It was a fleeting thought, and I quickly called Carl back.

"What the FUCK, Dan?" Carl shouted into his phone.

"I don't have time to explain," I said, "Just trust me, guy."

"Trust is wearing thin, Dan. You're acting REALLY strange. Is Anna trying to dump you or something?"

"It's wilder than that," I said, "I'm on my way to Pedro's in a cab right now. Can you still see Anna?"

"That's what I was trying to tell you, Dan when you **hung up on me!**"

"Jesus, Dan. Get with the program. Minutes matter."

"She was with someone. I couldn't see the person, but I could see her silhouette. It was definitely her, and she was standing with someone. It seemed like a man from the way he moved, but I can't be sure. They were outside the restaurant."

"Can you be any more vague?" I demanded, angry with myself for feeling jealous about her being with a mystery man.

"Give me a break, man, you asked me to follow Eve and some Latino dude, and now it's Anna and some guy? Get real! I'm not a detective for hire," Carl sounded frustrated. I had to tell him.

"Carl, Mom, Roberta and Eve are in danger. If we don't bring Anna to them, I'll be responsible for whatever happens to them," I pleaded with him.

"Seriously dude? You're going 5150 on me. Do we need to make you an appointment with a shrink?" Carl laughed.

"Believe me. It's bad. I got them into this; I have to get them out. Where did Anna and the mystery man go?"

At this point, the Lift driver was letting me off in front of Pedro's. At least I wasn't alone anymore. I leaped out of the car and into Pedro's.

Carl was sitting facing the main entrance with a clear view of who was coming and going munching on chips and salsa and drinking a Corona.

"Carl!" I shouted as I flew through the door and landed in a chair across from him.

"Careful, Dan. You're obscuring my view!" Carl said, chuckling, "I need to see Anna and the mystery man."

"Did they leave?" I asked, "I have to find them."

"There they are right now," Carl said, waving to a table across the room. I looked over and saw Anna, seated at a table talking to a man. I jumped up and ran to the table.

My jaw dropped.

Anna was having dinner with my dad.

EIGHTEEN

Anna had her back turned to me. My dad looked up, genuinely surprised at me.

"Daniel, come here and meet Frances."

Frances? I wondered why she was using a different name but not enough to avoid confronting her.

"Anna? What are you doing here?" I asked. She turned to me with those lovely translucent blue eyes. I had been intimate with this woman more than once. I knew this was Anna.

She said, "I'm sorry, I think you have me confused with someone else." She extended her arm and hand to me with those long, lovely nails, painted pink this time, but unmistakably the same.

"I'm Frances," she said, "And you're Daniel?"

How long was this farce going to continue?

Dad was sitting back with a skeptical expression on his face. It brought a lot of questions to mind.

"Frances is a financial expert," Dad was explaining, "She's going to make a trip to Europe for one of the companies I manage to meet up with our contact over there who oversees the operation to see if we can maximize profits. We may have to do some cutting, but before we do, we want Frances' expert opinion."

I'd never known what it was like to be in the twilight zone, but today I was no stranger. If it hadn't been for all the other ludicrous activities of the day, I might have come unglued, but I knew I had to be strong for everyone's safety. I was also deeply hurt by Anna's betrayal, pretending not to know me and working my dad? I had to stay in this long enough to sort it out.

"It's a pleasure," Anna said, sipping a glass of iced tea. I also noticed she was eating chicken enchiladas. So much for being vegan ruse.

I pulled up a chair to buy myself some time. I needed to get Anna to go back to the place where my mother, Roberta & Eve were all being held hostage, so I didn't want to blow this up and have my dad think I was the crazy one.

When I moved closer to the table, I saw a couple beads of sweat form on Anna/Frances' brow, and I realized she was "sweating", literally. She could pretend to be calm and collected, but it was nothing more than that: an act.

"I need to run to the rest room," Dad said, standing up. He smiled, "It'll give you two a chance to get acquainted." He left the table.

It was the chance I had been waiting for.

I grabbed Anna's arm, "What are you doing? Who are you pretending to be?"

"Please remove your hands, Dan. You can't do this here," she said calmly.

"You've put people's lives at risk. My mom and her friends are being held captive by those people who kidnapped me, and now I'm thinking you know more about them than you were letting on!" My voice was getting louder, and my temper was close to erupting.

"Dan, keep your cool. You're going to make this worse," Anna begged.

"Worse for who? You're eating lunch with my dad? Do you have something going on with him, too?"

She shot me a cold stare, "Your father is a business associate, and if I'd known you were his son, I never would have gotten involved with you."

"Seriously? You want to put this on me. You're changing identities, sneaking around pretending to be different people. You're eating chicken for God's sake; you're supposed to be a vegan!" I was losing it yet trying to be rational.

"I'm not who you think I am," Anna/Frances whispered.

"Gee, do you think? That's the first truthful thing you've said to me," I had officially lost it.

"Here's the thing, Anna, you have to pull it together enough to rescue my friends," I was referring to myself in terms of pulling it together, but I projected that feeling onto her. I was desperate.

"I'm not Anna," she said, "I'm Frances."

"That's convenient," I remarked snidely, "How do we get out of this one?" I asked.

"You'll have to lie low," she said, "Wait for me to call after I complete this assignment for your dad."

"You've **GOT** to be kidding me," I exploded, "You have no room to negotiate with me." I was boiling over.

"Please," Frances begged, "I need you to do this for me."

I didn't know who she was at this point, and I wasn't so sure what she was doing with my dad was on the up and up. I was tired of being complicit in covert activities. It wasn't me, and I wasn't going to do it.

"Anna, you can't ask me to do that."

"I'm not Anna," she whispered again, "Call me Frances."

"Okay, Frances, but you seemed ok with Anna when you were fucking me." I couldn't help it. I had lost all self-control.

My Dad was on his way back to the table, and I knew if we were going to say or do something, we had to make it fast.

At that moment, Igor burst into the restaurant with a police officer in uniform. They walked up to our table, and the police officer said, "Anna Hobart, also known as Frances Douglas, you are under arrest on suspicion of espionage," the stocky Latino police officer sandwiched himself between me and Igor and spread his legs so I couldn't get near her, although I was frozen in place and wasn't trying to intervene.

"You have the right to remain silent. Anything you say can and will be used against you in a court of law. You have the right to an attorney.

If you cannot afford an attorney, one will be provided for you. Do you understand the rights I have just read to you?"

Anna looked up at him, looked over at me and just stared her cool, calculated, emotionless stare, but somehow it seemed sad to me. More than sad, it felt tragic.

"Yes," she acknowledged.

Igor came up behind me and said, "Good job, Dan. Wearing that wire helped us track you. I was actually following you the whole time, not threatening the women."

It was a little late for me to feel relieved about that.

My dad had taken a few steps back when the cops showed up, and now he was again approaching us.

"Mr. Heller, we just arrested Frances Douglas on charges of espionage. It looks like we just saved your organization from doing business with an imposter."

Dad looked puzzled, and he directed his gaze to me. I just shrugged. None of this made sense to me. By this time, Carl had joined the party. He stood behind us watching intently, and for the first time I could remember in our entire relationship, he didn't say a word.

I wanted to say good-bye to Anna. I wanted to hug her. I was angry with her, and I felt betrayed and lied to, but I still had feelings for her. Conflict cursed through my veins. I didn't get a chance to say or do anything. Anna was looking down, handcuffed, and the officer was taking her away.

I watched without comment. The woman of my dreams wasn't who I thought she was, and she was walking out of life forever. I wanted to scream her name. I wanted to break down and cry, but instead, I did nothing at all. I just stood there.

And then my dad said, "Where's your mother?" and it jolted me out of stupor.

"Igor?" I asked.

"They're all fine. We were never going to harm them. Natasha and I work for the police department helping track down Russian criminals.

We were threatening you because we knew we were getting close, and we needed your help. The three women are with Frank and Natasha back where we met with you. We unhandcuffed them when you left," he explained.

I didn't know what to believe anymore. Had Anna been an animal rights activist or was that all part of her ruse? Had she extorted money from the restaurant or Don or caused the business any harm? Was Raj really her fiancé? Did she have multiple personalities? Was Anna really Frances or was she someone else entirely? And the worst question of all: why me? Why did I have to get entwined with her? My life as I knew it was hanging by a thread.

Dad, Carl, and I were escorted by Igor to the building where Mom, Roberta & Eve were actually not being held hostage. Frank was still flirting with Eve; Roberta had become her old self again, shouting, "Boy, do I have a story to tell the girls!" My mom just came running over to hug me.

"I was so worried about you, Dan," she said, "I know you have strong feelings for that girl, and she's in real trouble."

I was still processing, and at some level, deep inside, I was relieved that Mom, Roberta and Eve were all ok. I couldn't believe that Natasha and Igor were working for the police force. But at the same time, it made me more distraught about Anna. How could I have fallen for her? I felt duped. I felt used. I was still in love with her.

After we got home and Mom had gone to bed, Dad came out to the kitchen to talk.

"You know, Dan, you did a brave thing," he began.

"Brave? I fell in love with a con woman!" I yelled.

"You saved us from a catastrophe. I was going to send her to London to work with one of my top companies, and Dan, there would have been no coming back from the harm she would have caused our finances. She was probably going to leak all of our confidential information to some of her handlers in Russia."

"Dad, I doubt it's that nefarious."

"Really? You don't think it's a big deal that this woman was pretending to be someone she wasn't and getting involved in our financial dealings?"

By this time, I had checked the bank accounts for the restaurant and called to make sure Anna no longer had access. I had also verified that the funds hadn't been touched, and there was no evidence of tampering.

"I think she was just doing her job."

"Her job?" my dad asked, surprised.

"Yeah, I think she was working for someone in Russia, and it was her job to do what she did. To pretend she was Anna or Frances or whoever she introduced herself to us as and do whatever they told her to do. I really got that she was frightened and in over her head."

"She seemed pretty cool mannered to me," Dad commented, "I think she pulled the wool over your eyes."

I looked down and pondered the situation from beginning to end. My life with Anna in a nutshell.

"I don't think so, Dad. She is strong and confident, but she was just doing what she thought she had to do, pretending to be the personas her boss told her to. She must have been some kind of spy. I saw something else in her, but I was wrong. Maybe she was playing me, but I learned something from it," I reasoned.

"What's that?" Dad was authentically curious.

"I want to be vegan. I don't want to run a steakhouse or even be in the prime meats arena. I want to do something meaningful, like work with Mom and Roberta and Eve in the vegan cooking school business. I think it has real potential, and I want to work with people I know and trust."

I was surprised this all came to the forefront for me. Even several weeks ago, I wouldn't have had a clue what I wanted.

"You've grown up, Dan. I'm proud of you."

Here I was feeling like my heart was being ripped out of my chest, and my parents were proud of me; the police thought I had saved the day, and I hadn't destroyed the business I was involved in; in fact, I might have improved profitability over thirty percent, and I might be in the vegan cooking school business as a new career.

I knew I wasn't going to sleep well.

Nineteen

I had nightmares about Anna. She was running and jumping off a cliff, and I couldn't save her. I woke up in a sweat, and I realized the dream was accurate.

I called the police officer who made the arrest and asked to speak to her. He said I wasn't allowed to see her, but I could talk to her attorney, and he gave me the name.

I called the attorney and got a call back that afternoon. Her attorney's name was Nancy.

"Nancy, I'd like to talk to your client privately if I may," I requested.

"Given the circumstances," Nancy informed me, "That's a strange request."

"Would you just ask Anna? It's not about her case."

"You mean Frances, and yes, everything is about the case now."

I got her to agree to call me back with a definitive answer, not holding out my hope for a "yes." I just had to see Anna one last time.

I went to the dark kitchen, and I was surprised to find Eve back at work already.

"Hey, where's your mom?" I asked.

"Oh," she smiled, "She needed some time off to recover, and I think your mom's doing the same thing."

"Why not you?" I asked curiously.

"I need something to occupy my mind. There's this boy I can't get my mind off."

I laughed, "A boy named Dan?"

For some reason, she was looking more and more attractive to me. Could it be because she wasn't an international spy?

"It sure is. Would you even possibly consider a boring girl like me?"

"Why boring?" I asked, although I did sort of have that opinion of her.

"Well, compared to the illustrious ANNA ..."

"Don't even go there!" We both laughed, and then a wave of seriousness came over me, "I learned my lesson. Enough said."

Of course, it didn't end there. I was still processing, and that afternoon when Nancy called me back, I was delighted to learn that Anna was willing to talk to me one last time.

I met her in the holding area at the jail. She was in a protected room with a headset, and I was outside the glass partition. I was told we had five minutes to talk. She looked glum, especially without makeup, but she had that same resolve I had come to love. She was pale and stoic, but she hadn't been crying. She looked rock solid: unshaken.

"I know you can't tell me much," I admitted, "but is there anything you want to say?"

She looked up at me, "It's not personal, Dan," she said.

"Not personal?" I looked away. I was in love with a woman who didn't think it was "personal." At the same time, I didn't want to lay a guilt trip on her at our last meeting ever.

"I enjoyed getting to know you, even though I'm not Anna, and you see, there was never any future for us. That's why it was always just fun and games."

"But the veganism wasn't that. You took me to that disgusting hen house! You were passionate about the cause!"

"It was all part of the identity I assumed, Dan. Now the people I work for will try to get me out of this, and it may work. I may be back in Russia before you know it."

I just stared at her. How could someone be so heartless? Didn't she realize she was messing with people's lives?

"Was Raj really your fiancé?" I asked.

"He was a mark."

"And my dad?"

"The same."

Anna was your basic criminal. Or Frances. And there wasn't anything "basic" about it.

"Why?" I asked, pleaded, demanded, "Why me?"

Before Anna could answer, I heard a loud beeping sound, and our time had come to an end. Anna was taken away, and I had to come to terms with the realization that I would never see her again.

I walked out with more questions than answers.

❦ TWENTY

TEN YEARS LATER

"Hurry up!" Eve shouted. She was carrying a large tray of appetizers and wanted me to bring around the drink tray. We had a Cuban vegan restaurant in Tampa, and the two of us were running it together. Elliott, the vegan guy I had met in NYC at the steakhouse had funded us.

Carl was the numbers guy, making sure we turned an impressive profit, and Carl was also helping to run the place. We had a couple of large parties tonight, and the place was packed. I was running around madly, refilling drinks, checking on the cooks, and making sure the waiters had everything they needed.

Don Price came in with a beautiful woman on his arm. She was blond and lovely, trim, and elegant. She reminded me of Anna.

I seated the two of them at one of our most coveted tables with a view of the busy street below.

"You and Eve make a great couple," Don said, "But I have to tell you, I really miss you and Carl running the business."

"We miss it, too, but at least we got profits up for you," I reminded him.

"Of course," he said, "No hard feelings."

I took their orders personally, and as I walked away, I said, "You'll have to come by and meet our daughter some time. Her name is Jezebel, but we call her Jessie."

I was proud of my three-year-old, and my mother was delighted to have a grandchild.

"Of course," Don said, hesitating, as if he wanted to say something more.

I watched him explain to his date that he needed to talk to me privately, and then he grabbed my arm and took me aside to the bar area. Leaning against a cocktail table, he asked, "Have you heard anything more about Anna?"

Don had heard the whole story from my dad, painting me as the hero, and at the time, Don had just been thrilled he hadn't been the victim of her espionage activities.

"No, nothing," I admitted. I had deliberately distanced myself.

"Rumor has it," Don confided in me, lowering his voice to a whisper, "that she got out without jail time. Somehow there was a prisoner exchange with Russia, and then she may have changed identities again and disappeared."

"Wow! Well, you are more on top of things than I'll ever be. You must be well connected."

"Just thought I'd let you know!" Dan told me, adding, "Love this place. Great food! You're the man!"

I took a moment to reflect on my life. Things had turned out well in the end. I'd had my fling with Anna, who wasn't even her real identity, and Eve had given me another chance, and I'd discovered that she was a dedicated life partner, a loving mother, and a committed business partner. What else does a man need?

Carl called out to me, "Hey, Dan, you're never going to believe this!" He ran towards me with a piece of flan to try on a small plate.

"You're yelling at me over flan?" I asked.

"Hardly. That was just what I had in my hand. Look over there!"

He pointed in the direction of the door, and my heart stopped.

It was Anna.

She stood in the door, looking ten years older from the fine lines on her face and the mature hair style, but still as majestic and elegant as ever, understated, self-controlled but commanding.

She was dressed in black satin with a colorful silk scarf. I just stared, frozen in place, immovable.

Then a man walked up behind her, encircled her shoulders with his arm, and put in his name at the hostess station.

After they were seated, I told the hostess I'd take their table.

Anna recognized me immediately. I knew by the slight gleam in her eyes, and then with just a flicker, it was gone, and she went stoic again.

"I'll have a steak," her dinner companion said.

"We don't serve steak," I replied, "If you are a carnivore, you'll have to go somewhere else."

He gave me a distasteful grimace, "Can you believe that, chérie? No steak at a gourmet restaurant?"

"You know what they say," Anna replied, "Nobody goes to a steakhouse looking for a Brussels sprout pizza."

Our eyes met, and in that moment, the world stood still. It was ten years earlier; I was ten years younger, and we were back in NYC. We stared into each other's eyes.

"Whatever happened to Cruella?" I asked.

"Oh, you know, cats, they just run away," she said.

Her dinner companion looked at me strangely, and then at her, and then back to me.

"Do you two know each other?"

"Of course, not," I replied, "Just trying to make conversation." I hoped I didn't give her away. I had no ill intent. I was astonished to see her again, and I was no longer hurt or angry. I was grateful for the opportunity to know firsthand that someone I had loved and lost was thriving, even if she was just a common thief.

I touched base with Carl, "The flan was great. Add it to our dessert menu!" He smiled. "How was she?" He was dying to know how our conversation went.

"Same old Anna," I replied.

I went to restroom and then planned to head back to work, but as I was standing at the urinal, a woman walked in and stood in the doorway.

"Is there a private room here?" she asked.

I looked up and saw Anna.

"Actually, a stall will do," she added.

She paused.

I didn't reply.

She said, "We have a lot in common, you know. We both like to fuck."

www.ingramcontent.com/pod-product-compliance
Lightning Source LLC
Chambersburg PA
CBHW071319130726
47996CB00002B/539